The Thornhaired Princess

Brett McCoy

Copyright © 2016 by Brett McCoy

All rights reserved. This book or any portion thereof may not be reproduced or used in any manner whatsoever without the express written permission of the publisher except for the use of brief quotations in a book review.

Chapter 1

The Gardener's Daughter

The gardener's daughter had an unusual name. Not just unusual for a girl, like Mike or Brian or Curtis, but unusual for anyone.

Her name was Pocket, a name her father had chosen as he had chosen everything else for his daughter since the day she was born, the day his wife, her mother, passed away.

Pocket's ten years had been good though, even without a mother, for her father was a good man but was also something else entirely. He was a gardener of a most unusual sort.

They lived in a quaint house in the village of Sail, which sat a couple miles west of the Great River and home to several dozen perfectly lovely people. Pocket cherished her time in Sail especially time spent in her father's garden.

The garden was a large patch of earth in the back of their house. Pocket had measured it as accurately as she knew how. It was five two-footed hops across and seven giant-steps long. Her father worked the garden every day and everyday Pocket watched.

He walked through the garden in a very odd fashion. He'd visit each plant and appear to talk to them. He'd bend down to whisper to plants that only reached up to his knees or above. Plants only up to Pocket's ankles or toes were treated a little differently. He'd kneel on the ground to whisper to those, which was why his pants had patches all around the knees.

The Thornhaired Princess

Pocket knew he wasn't talking to the plants, not really. He was singing to them, singing a very special song. This song, his gardener's song, is what made her father such an unusual gardener.

While he grew berry bushes, and pepper plants, those were not the only things in the garden. Sure there were tomatoes and carrots, but there was so much more. In one corner there was lettuce and in another he'd started a watermelon vine, but there were other things in between, things found in no other garden in the world.

Amongst all the green leaves and colorful fruits, there were other things. Things not for eating.

This garden grew glass and iron and cloth from seeds all their own.

"Come here, Pocket," the gardener called. "It's time I taught you to Grow."

Pocket raced from the porch at the back of the house and with seven giant-steps she reached her father in the garden.

"Really?" Pocket asked, full of glee. "You're going to teach me?"

"Of course, I can't be expected to grow everything myself. Not forever anyway."

Pocket knew that was true enough. She had always wanted to learn her father's growing song but knew it was a secret for him alone to keep. Now she would learn and it would be a wonderful treat.

Her father led her to a patch of empty soil. There was not much of that left in the garden this time of year, but it looked as if he'd been saving this spot for just this occasion. An empty little square sat far off in the corner alone and prepared for something new to go there.

"Take this," he said, handing Pocket a small seed. "This is for an apple tree."

"A whole tree?" Pocket asked.

"Why yes, but this is a special kind of apple tree. This one will only grow a bit taller than me."

"Well that's still pretty tall."

The Thornhaired Princess

"I suppose it is, compared to you."

Pocket took the seed and went to the empty soil.

"Dig a small hole as deep as your hand. When the hole is complete, drop in the seed."

She did as he instructed. When she dropped in the seed, she waited.

"Now, cover it up with the dirt."

Again, she did as she was told.

"Now, here is the part you have yet to learn." He came over next to her and knelt down in the soft soil. Even though she didn't have to, Pocket did the same. She wanted to be close to the song so she didn't miss a word.

Her father began to sing and she felt so warm. Never before had she been close enough to hear the words, but hear them she did. They were not like normal words and she didn't see how she would ever learn them. They were more like feelings. They felt the way she did when she heard birds sing, or when she listened to the wind in the trees. Some parts were like listening to the colors of the rainbow. It was a beautiful song.

"Now you try," her father said.

She did as she was told. She sung as best she could. She didn't think she was doing it right and it took all her concentration. She knew it would take time to learn so she didn't get up her hopes. She looked to her father when she finished but he was looking over her shoulder and down, down to the ground.

There in the soil where she'd planted the seed, was a small shoot already popping through the ground, the start to the tree.

"Very good, Pocket," he said. "You're a quick learner."

"Surely not, father," she said. "It must have been your words that did this, not mine."

But he shook his head. "It is the one that planted the seed who must sing the song of growing."

"Really?" Pocket asked.

"Really," her father said. "Congratulations, daughter, you're a

Grower and a gardener!"

They hugged there, both kneeling in the garden.

They stood and made their way towards the house. As they went Pocket paused looking at something in the garden. It was a large unusual plant that wasn't a plant at all. It was sheets of glass all connected at their edges like walls. The sections branched off one another the same way that ice forms on top of the ponds in winter.

"Father?" Pocket asked.

"Yes, dear.?

"When do I get to learn how to grow glass?"

He laughed a terrific laugh. "Why daughter, you already know how. In fact, I just taught you. It is the same song that grows the apple trees and carrots that grows glass. It is the song of growing, after all. To grow something different or unusual you just need an unusual seed."

"Oh, I see," Pocket said.

"But be careful, daughter, for the song of growing works in strange ways and you must be prepared to harvest whatever it is you plant."

"I will be careful, father, of course I will."

"Come in for dinner now, there will be plenty of time to practice more tomorrow."

"That will be grand."

The gardener and his daughter with the unusual name went in for dinner. All the while the gardener's daughter smiled, beaming with joy. She would be careful as she had told her father, but she could not wait to tell her friend Wick, the boy who worked in his mother's shop making candlesticks.

Chapter 2

The Candlemaker's Son

"Hello, and welcome to The Wickerson Candle Shop! I'm Wick Wickerson," Wick said. Wick was the son of the candle shop owner and candlemaker.

"Good to see you, Wick," said the customer. "How is your mother doing?"

"She's great," Wick said. "Do you need any help finding anything?"

"Maybe. Do you have any new colors today?"

"Not today, I'm afraid. But I heard from a little birdie that there might be some later this week."

"Oh really?" said the customer.

"Yes, but the birdie also talked a lot about worms and bugs so you never know."

The customer chuckled and continued around the shop.

Wick enjoyed working in the store most days, but what he really liked was working in the shop with his mother. Those were the great days. Just sitting in there as she worked her magic putting the candles together was nothing but joy. All the scents and different colors, it was really something to see.

When the store closed for the day he went into the back room where his mother sat looking through a large book. This book held all the family recipes for candles she'd already made and blank pages for the ones she would in the future.

"How was business today?" she asked.

"You were only gone for an hour, mother, you know how it went."

"Maybe that was an important hour."

"No, it was not. I did my best to let people know about your new work so hopefully more will come soon."

"Oh they will. This will be my best yet. Ready to help?"

"Of course!"

They worked well into the night. Luckily they had plenty of candles to light up the workshop! Wick's mother did the mixing of the ingredients as Wick prepped the molds and wicks. It was fun work especially when working with his mother.

Once the first batch hardened they did their first test. Wick slid the candle from the mold and handed it to his mother.

"I think you can do this one," she said. "After all, you helped."

"Thanks, mother."

He took the matches and struck one across the work bench. He lit the candle and waited. When it started to burn the wax the flame changed colors from the common yellow to a bright, glassy gold.

"Very nice," he said.

"Glad you like it, but give it a minute."

He waited at his mother's suggestion as the candle burned its bright gold. The flame stayed the same but something else came off of it. The smoke trailing off was a nice white, but the scent is what really stood out.

"What is that?" Wick asked.

"Think," his mother said. "You'll figure it out."

So he did. Wick smelled and rattled his brain trying to figure it out. Then it clicked.

"It's apple pie," he said. Then with another sniff added, "With cinnamon."

"Quite right," his mother said, smiling at her son.

"It's lovely, mother."

"Well, you can have that one and add it to your collection. I'm sure you don't have a gold candle for your tricks, unless I'm mistaken?"

"Of course not, mother."

"Well now you do."

They cleaned up the workshop and returned home. Despite it being a bit late Wick wasn't tired at all. In fact, he'd been energized with a new candle at his disposal and couldn't wait to test it out.

See his mother may be the candlemaker, but Wick was a candle *artist*. He had at least one of every one of his mother's candles somewhere stored away. He always got one from the test batch and kept them close. He had several more of his favorites which he kept with a box of matches in a satchel.

He grabbed that satchel and headed back outside. He made his way down the street passing Pocket's house, heading towards the farms at the north part of Sail. There he set down his collection and pulled out two of his favorites, the fountain water blue, and the new cinnamon gold. Those weren't the official names, just how he knew them.

He lit both and waited for them to burn their special colors. Once he did he started to *draw* with their flames in the air.

The special thing about Wick's drawings is that they stayed up in the air, hanging there as if the flame-light had frozen in place. It lasted only a few moments, but it was an unusual sight for sure.

"Pretty," said a voice from behind. It was a small voice, bright and cheerful. As always it brought a smile to his face.

"Hello, Pocket," Wick said. "How did you know I was here?"

"Your mother told me she had given you a new candle. I wouldn't dare miss a show like that?"

Wick shrugged.

"Go on, go on, I want to see more pretty things!"

Wick drew and drew, each picture seeming to float around until they'd stayed just long enough. Then puff, they went out with a small outlines of smoke. With each one Pocket clapped and cheered.

The Thornhaired Princess

The candles eventually burned and Wick was tired as well, he sat down next to his friend who'd been entranced with his spell. Drawing was tough work, especially with the flames of candles.

"I have some news of my own," Pocket said.

"Oh really," Wick said. "Let me guess, you're actually a pineapple?"

"No, dummy."

"Oh, well then you must have found a treasure map."

"Kind of," she said. "Only much, much better."

"I hardly think it's funny to joke about something being better than a treasure map."

"Fine, then just as good."

"You're going to have to convince me that's possible, but I'll let you try just this once."

"My father taught me his song of growing!"

"You don't look any taller."

"I'm going to kick you, Wick!"

Wick burst out laughing. "Of course I'm only joking. That's great news! And I will agree that is just as good as a treasure map, maybe even better!"

"Isn't it though?"

"So what are you going to grow?"

"That's the question now isn't it?" Pocket said with a wink.

"Well, what do you *want* to grow?"

"I don't know. There's just so much that can be done it too hard to choose."

"It's a good thing I'm here."

Pocket looked at him sideways. "Why? Do you have something you want grown?"

"No, but if you can't ever make up your mind I'll just have to tell you what to grow."

"Never would such a thing happen. Even if you did I would lie to myself and say it was my idea all along."

"I know you would and I would be fine with that, of course."

The Thornhaired Princess

"Of course," Pocket said, "what are friends for?"

Chapter 3

The Blue Marble

Sometime later that week, Pocket sat on her porch looking out over the garden. She had been reading a book, one of the few her father had been able to bring back from the city, but she'd given up. The bright sun and green leaves were too distracting, especially on such a warm day.

She sat looking out over the garden and her new tree. Its top leaves had already grown almost beyond her reach, even when she was on her tippy-toes.

That's when she saw it. Along near the edge of her garden, a cute little squirrel hopped right on by.

Squirrels, her father always said, could be troublesome or helpful. She'd have to keep a close eye to see which this one would be. She watched it hop this way and that. Every time it paused it looked around as if it was up to no good. It hopped a couple more times, and then a few more after that. It seemed to have found something this time as it stopped and did not look around, but down into the soil, digging underground.

It scurried its paws into the soil and came up with something unexpected and quite unusual. It its little paws where usually only acorns or berries were found, was a small round ball colored a sunset sky-blue.

"What have you found there?" Pocket said out loud.

The squirrel didn't reply of course, unless its reply was to hop out of the garden, towards the farms beyond.

"Hey! Wait! You can't steal that!" She was only joking of course, but she chased after it all the same.

The squirrel bounded this way and that and Pocket followed. She would never catch the squirrel, that much she knew, but it was fun to try. Not to mention it was sunny and warm and what better things were there to do?

The squirrel eventually made its way to the Lancaster orchard where it scurried into a very tall peach tree. The peach trees were some of Pocket's favorite as they always flowered so lovely in spring, and the fuzzy peaches were always so sweet.

The squirrel came to rest halfway up the trunk. It was there, in a small nook between branches that it left the marble behind. The squirrel went on its way, forgetting its treasure, and Pocket looked up and accepted the challenge.

First she tried the easy way. She shook the tree as hard as she dared. She didn't want any peaches to fall. Shook as she might, the marble was locked in tight. There was nothing else to do now but climb.

She made her way carefully, making sure to find snug places for her hands and feet. It didn't seem so high up now that she was halfway there. With a few more careful steps, it would be within reach.

The marble sat just overhead with her last step. She reached up, grasping tight on a branch with her left hand and staying steady on her feet. She stretched and stretched and then stretched some more, until her hand closed around the marble so blue and so smooth.

"I've got you now," she said.

She climbed back down and leaned against the tree. "Hmm," she said. "I think this might make a most unusual seed."

She raced back to her house and into the garden. She searched and searched for a place to plant but then a smile broke across her face, a mischievous smile, a smile of tricksters and sneaks. A wonderful idea had popped into her mind, she'd make her very own garden starting with a tree of a most unusual kind.

She wondered through town, down its cobblestone avenue and down a few dirt paths looking for a perfect spot. She waved to the butcher, the baker, and the brewer with one hand as she carried her marble in the other. She continued down the road until she found the right place.

Far at the end of town, where the cobblestones end was a large perfect space. She knew what it was for, of course, it was where the old boat-maker had lived. The boat-maker had moved away a long time ago seeing as how business had been slow. Not much need for boats out here where there are only ponds and streams. But the house had remained and now sat rotting. Inside would be an interesting and unusual place for a private garden.

She ducked inside, which wasn't hard since there was no door, and she found a spot to plant her marble where there wasn't any floor.

She planted it in some soft wet soil and sang the song of growing. She waited and waited until a tiny blue stalk grew from the ground.

Pocket laughed and laughed and laughed all the way home. Her father would be so proud, her making a garden all her own.

She went to bed smiling and maybe laughing some more. When she woke something had happened that was most unusual for sure.

She got out of bed when her father's voice flew in through the window. "Pocket, dear, come outside please."

Once outside she found a large crowd gathered at the end of the cobblestone street, standing in front of the old boat-maker's house, all looking up.

Cracking through the roof of the boat-maker's old house large blue tree limbs with leafless branches and baring unusual fruit. On the end of the branches were blue rods as long as her arms all shiny like brand new blue glass.

"Pocket, dear, it seems that you were seen going into that house yesterday by the butcher, the baker, and the brewer."

"Yes, I did go in," Pocket said.

"And?"

"And I planted a blue marble I found."

"I see," her father said.

"Well, it seems that the marble wasn't a marble at all, but an earring made of blue diamond in a granite setting."

"Oh boy!" Pocket said.

"Oh boy, indeed," Her father said, but not looking to keen.

"What do we do with diamonds and granite?"

"Diamonds have value of a kind, as you know, Pocket, and granite is good for building certain things, but finding someone who can work with it is tough to find."

"Not to worry," said a voice. It came from a large-armed man with dust covering a big black apron. Pocket knew him like everyone in town. He was the stonemason, and a jolly guy all around. "I have worked with granite, and with the easy access to diamond, this will be a cinch."

"If you say so," Pocket's father said.

It was lots of hard work and everyone in town started to help, but soon the tree became as commonplace as any of the buildings or people in town.

Over the next few months it attracted a great deal of extra business into town, most coming from the city of Vent, a large busy place a short ways up the river. New people came daily to get the wares made from Pocket's tree, and it made her and her father quite wealthy indeed. Of course, her father never liked having too much, so he shared his new wealth with the town, letting all sorts of new things come into their little village. If things continued like this the town might not end up so small after all.

"That was a neat thing you made," Wick told Pocket one day.

"It was nothing, really," Pocket said. "But really we should find that squirrel."

"A squirrel?"

"Oh yes. We have to find him and thank him! Without his good luck I would have never found that lovely unusual seed."

"OK then," Wick said. "Thank you, squirrel, wherever you are!"

Chapter 4

The Sky Puppets

A few years snuck by and the town of Sail continued growing and thriving in no small part to Pocket's new tree. The blue tree attracted new people, both for the material and as a site to beyond. A good number of them stayed, making Sail their home. The cobblestone was extended, looping around the old house with the blue tree sticking through it with more houses and shops opening beyond.

"It's quite nice, the blue tree," Wick said one day.

Pocket was Wick were out for a walk, heading to the new shops. "It really is. And to think I thought planting that marble might lead to nothing but trouble."

That had a good laugh at that.

One of the new shops that had opened in town was a place that created a new kind of lunch food and sold it. It was very popular. The shop was owned by a woman named Viera and her shop was called "Viera's Sandwiches".

The first time Pocket had gone to eat there she couldn't believe such a place existed. "Who in their right mind would ever eat sand?" she had asked.

Wick had shrugged.

The Thornhaired Princess

But it turns out the sandwiches were very delightful and Viera made almost as many types of sandwiches as Wick's mother made candles.

Today they were going to try something new, Pocket hoped.

They made their way up to the shop and got in line. There was always a line at Viera's and had been ever since she'd built the place.

They went up to the counter and there was Viera. She was a tall woman with short hair, but not really short. It hung down to about her chin.

"Hello children," she said.

"We're not children anymore," Pocket said. "I'm twelve now."

"Quite right," Viera said. "Would a young lady such as you like to try something new?"

"Of course I would," Pocket said.

Viera went back out of sight for a brief moment and came back with an unusual sandwich for both Pocket and Wick. There was bread, of course, but no meat of any kind nor was there any cheese.

"Are you sure this is a sandwich," Wick asked.

"Isn't the name of this place 'Viera's Sandwiches'?" Viera asked.

Wick smiled and took a bite. "Well it's quite good, Pocket."

Pocket took a bite. It was good, but whatever the gooey stuff in the center was stuck to the roof of her mouth quite a bit.

"Wha' i' dis'?" she asked, mouth full of bread the sticky stuff.

"It's called peanut butter!" Viera said. "Here, you need this, too."

She handed them each a glass of creamy milk. With a swig Pocket flushed down the sticky sandwich.

"This is very good," Pocket said.

"I'm very glad you like it. Since you were willing to try it I'll let you have these for free." She leaned over the counter and whispered, "Just don't let old Turin over there know that. I made him pay for his."

"Well he is quite crabby," Wick said.

"Have you talked with him today?" Pocket asked.

"No, but I don't need to," Wick said. "He's always crabby."

The Thornhaired Princess

Pocket and Wick went outside to eat on one of the tables on the shop's patio. It was a gloriously sunny day, a good one for eating outdoors.

They ate slowly, savoring the peanut butter sandwiches. Pocket licked her fingers as she polished off her last bite. When she looked up in delight a giant cloud rolled overhead, covering them and the entire village in a sea of shadow.

"Where did such a big cloud come from so suddenly?" Wick asked.

But when they both looked up to see the big cloud they discovered something troubling.

The big cloud wasn't, in fact, a cloud at all.

They had heard stories, of course, by now everyone had. The sky city on a great island in the sky had been seen here and there, though they'd never heard of it coming so close to a town. And why here to Sail? Surely a city that could fly would have no need to visit a small village such as there's.

The shadow moved and hovered until the island came to a rest. It was hard to say for sure, but if Pocket had to guess it had stopped with its center straight over the divider between the old part of Sail and the new. Straight over her lovely blue tree.

Once it stopped dozens of smaller shadows appeared at the edges. Shapes high above were seen floating and falling towards the ground.

Practically everyone in Sail had come running out towards the blue tree. They'd all come to see what this great shadow was and now that they'd seen it some were too scared to leave.

"What is it doing here?" Someone cried out.

Pocket watched, waiting as the first of the little falling shapes came into view. They looked like people, at first, but when they landed she saw they were not people at all. While they had arms and legs and heads and bodies like people, they had something else, something extra that made them unlike people in one very important way.

Each and every one swung down from the island dangling from strings.

"How do they stay untangled?" Wick asked, almost talking to himself.

"Oh no," came another cry. "It's really them. The puppet pirates are here!"

True enough that's what they were, Pocket saw. They were puppets, not people at all. These puppets raced around the house with the blue tree, swarming all around it like flies on fallen fruit.

"We are here," said a loud booming voice. It came from everywhere and nowhere all at once. It just was, loud and echoing. "We come for the tree!"

"No!" Pocket cried.

A group of men, the butcher, the baker, and the brewer, were there and looked ready to fight these puppets away. Others gathered as well. The butcher looked ferocious with his big meat cleaver. The baker hand a big pot and roller for bashing. The brewer had his big metal spoon that looked enough like a sword for Pocket's pleasure. But she had nothing but her peanut butter sandwich and as yummy as it was it would be no help in a battle.

She had to watch as the men raced in towards the puppets. But the puppets were quick and were pulled upward out of reach. They swooped in like birds, knocking the men flying. More and more of the townsfolk rushed out to help. The butcher got lucky and with a miss, the swing cut the strings to one of the puppets sending it tumbling. It went down to the ground in a heap and a rumbling. There was a cheer for that but really it mattered very little. The puppets were too many, and too quick, and they never grew tired.

"It is no use," said the voice. "Do not fight us and we will not hurt you. Just let us take the tree and we will be on our way."

More strings came down, bigger ones than those for the puppets. The puppets wrapped them around the tree and gave them all a nice tug. With these ropes secure a loud noise blasted from the floating island above. The ropes went tighter and then tighter still. The tree began to shake and shiver. Pocket could only watch in horror as the great blue tree was ripped from the house and the ground all around and hoisted into the air, up to the floating island in the sky.

"Where are they taking my tree?" Pocket yelled.

"Wherever they want," said a voice from behind. It was her father, the gardener, Pocket saw. He looked sad and weary.

"But why?" Pocket asked.

"Because it was good, and nice, and they are thieves. That's just what thieves do."

The whole town of Sail stood outside looking off to the east as the island floated away. The tree hung below for quite a long time before it finally made its way up to the island and slid out of view.

"What are we going to do?" Pocket asked.

"As we have always done," her father said. "We will continue to plant new seeds from which new things will grow."

Chapter 5

Beyond the Cobblestone Road

Her father's words gave Pocket a small bit of hope, but only the tiniest of bits. The tree had brought so much joy and new friends and even though she thought of it as hers in some ways it belonged to the town. Without the tree she would have never had peanut butter and that made her sad. What else would she miss out on now? Those evil pirate puppets were making her quite mad.

"Those lousy pirates!" she yelled to Wick. "We can't let them get away with this!"

Wick said nothing. He did not know what they could do.

The town continued on for a few days before it showed any real sign of change. People continued to come, though now they wanted to see where the tree *had* been, instead of seeing it proper. But Pocket knew that would not last, seeing nothing is never as nice as seeing *something*.

"We will survive without the tree," her father said at dinner. "We were fine before, we'll be fine again."

"Will we?" Pocket asked. "What of the new people? Will they stay?"

"Perhaps. Perhaps not. Change is the way of the world. You just have to make memories and be with people while you can, and when they leave you'll still have those memories close at hand."

The Thornhaired Princess

"I liked it better with the tree," Pocket said. "Now it seems empty."

Despite her father's words, the town started to suffer. Fewer people were coming through Sail which meant fewer shoppers at the new shops. Pocket and her father were fine as they had saved quite a bit during the days of the blue tree. They even had enough to help out some of the other people here and there. But that would eventually have to stop, too, and everyone knew it.

"Viera's Sandwiches" was not the first to close, but close it did. She packed up and headed east for one of the bigger cities to try and open again.

Pocket went out for walk when she heard that news. She walked by the closed up shop and could barely keep herself from weeping. Had she caused this trouble to come to Sail? Perhaps without her making such a fuss those thieves would never have come. But the tree had caused the people to come in the first place so she would have missed the good stuff too.

"This is too much," she said. "Too much, too much, too much, I don't know what to do!"

Her walk led her to the now empty house where the tree once stood. She made herself go in and see where the roots of the great tree had been pulled out by that silly soaring island. Also inside, thrown down in the hole was that lone puppet the butcher had chopped clear of its strings. It looked kind of sad down there in the hole. Though of course she didn't feel sad for it at all.

"Don't tell me you're planting *that?*" said Wick. He had seen her from the street and had come to check to see if she was alright. But the snaking up on her gave her a small fright.

"No, silly. I'm not planting that puppet. I wouldn't want a whole tree of *those* evil things."

"Well then you should take it to the town hall tonight."

"The town hall? Whatever for?"

"I have an idea," Wick said. "But it might be kind of silly."

"Your ideas are never silly, Wick."

"I hope you're right."

Pocket hopped in the hole and scooped up the puppet. It was surprisingly light and easy to carry. They walked to the town hall together as Wick explained his idea. It was silly. Quite silly indeed, but it was also wonderful. So wonderful in fact that Pocket was angry all over again for not thinking of it herself.

The town hall was a large building on the north end of Sail. The elder townsfolk, such as Wick's mother and Pocket's father, were having a meeting regarding the state of affairs in the town now that the tree had been stolen. It wasn't really a place for them but Wick's idea, silly as it was, may be able to help the town.

They went inside, Wick now taking a turn carrying the puppet.

"Why have you brought that vile thing in here?" asked the mayor. The mayor was an older man, shorter than most in town, but he was known to be very smart indeed. He had planned the cobblestone road and had designed most of the houses in town.

"We would like to ask you all for a favor," Pocket said. "Wick has a plan."

Wick set the puppet down on the floor and approached the twenty or so people seated in the hall. "I would like you to allow Pocket and I to adventure out beyond Sail, to find the sky island and to trade this puppet for the tree."

The elders looked at Wick, confused.

"What makes you think they would trade the tree for this stringless puppet?" The baker asked.

"These puppets no matter who controls them are some sort of family, surely they would want one of their own returned," Wick said. "I would trade anything to bring one of you home."

His mother looked at him with pride. Pocket saw her father looking at her, clearly wondering what she might be up to with this little "adventure." The other elders though, kept their eyes on Wick, all of them thinking over his plan.

"I don't know, lad," the butcher said. "It's dangerous out there in many places. The things that haunt stories don't always stay in the pages of books."

"That is why we came to you for help first. We will need supplies and directions. But I think you know that we'll be going with or without your help, for this is something we must do."

Pocket tried her best to hide her surprise. This most certainly had *not* been part of his silly plan which had just become even sillier. But she kept that to herself or so she thought. Her father was still looking at her. Had he seen her shock? Hopefully not.

"So that's the way of it?" the mayor asked. "I suppose I shouldn't be surprised. You two are getting older, getting to where you want to see more of the world. I will be leaving this up to your parents, of course. If they agree to let this little adventure go forward, you will have any help the town can provide."

The attention turned toward Wick's mother and Pocket's father. Both sat quietly for a several minutes, each seeming to want the other go first. It was Pocket's father who stood and spoke first.

"You should go east until you reach the river. There you will find a way to reach where you need to go." He sat down. That, it seemed, had been enough to show his approval.

Wick's mother stood next. "I have new candles you may take, special ones you've never seen. They will help you in your travels."

She, too, took her seat.

The mayor stood third. "Good baker, Good butcher, prepare some traveling food for these two. They will need enough to last several days, I'm sure."

"Will do," said the butcher and the baker.

"Thank you," Wick said.

Pocket gave a curtsy and they headed out of the hall.

"Can you believe it?" Wick said. "We get to go on adventure!"

"I know," Pocket said, though feeling quite scared. "It will be lovely and grand."

"It will be most grand."

That very next morning Pocket found a bag of supplies waiting for her just by the front door of their house. Nearby the string-less puppet rested against the wall. Pocket looked through the pack and found some sausage and jerky from the butcher, and several tightly bound hunks of fresh bread from the baker. Her father had supplied some apples from their tree as well as a skin full of water.

He came into the front room of the house as she looked through the bag.

"Be careful out there, my dear. There are things out in the world worse than those puppets."

"I know, father, you have taught me well."

"I see that now. It is hard for us parents to know that sometimes."

Pocket gave her father a big warm hug.

With a glance in the bag she looked in and found…

"Father?"

"Yes, my love?"

"Why did you pack that broken old writing pen?"

Her father shrugged. "Just for luck, I suppose. Having that pen has led me to everything that has brought me joy. That's the pen that fell out of your mother's pocket that caused us to meet. Perhaps it will help you on this journey of yours."

"Well, thank you, father. I'm sure you are right."

She made her way to the door.

"One more thing before you go, dear. The tree is, at the end of it all, just a tree."

"Father?"

"Just remember that even if you don't get the tree, your adventure may not be a failure."

Pocket gave him a confused look. She didn't understand that at all, but didn't want to say so. "Of course, father."

He nodded. "Well, then. Off you go!"

Chapter 6

The Six-Handed Fisherman

Pocket and Wick made their way over the wide dirt road leading away from Sail. They came to a spot at the edge of the last farm, the very farthest piece of land that was still considered part of their home town.

"Here it is," Pocket said. "When we pass here we'll truly have gone."

"We're not gone, we're right here," Wick said.

"I know but I've never left home before."

"Isn't it exciting?"

"Maybe," Pocket said. "I'm not quite sure."

The truth was she was kind of scared. She liked Sail and loved her father and now that she knew how to grow things in the garden she had started to like it even more. Of course, there was a task ahead of them now, and an important one at that.

They walked straight until the sun was high overhead. Wick spotted a nice patch of low grass just over a hillside where they decided to take a lunch break. They sat in the grass and shared some the food the town had provided for them.

"It's a good day to start an adventure," Pocket said.

"It sure is."

"How long before we reach the river?"

Wick shook his head. "I'm not sure. I've only been once when my mother took me up to Vent to sell some of our candles. But that time we had a horse and a wagon so it didn't take so long as walking."

The break only lasted about twenty minutes before they resumed their journey. They crossed a number of grassy hills and hopped over trickling streams. All in all, it took them three more hours of walking before Pocket spotted the river.

"Look ahead, that little bright sliver!" she shouted.

Wick squinted to where Pocked stood pointing. Off in the distance he saw the small band of shimmering flecks as the water raced by. They were in sight of the Great River!

"We're still far off," Wick said.

"But it's getting closer!"

At last they arrived at the river. Its banks were muddy with small islands of clumped grass scattered throughout. The river was bigger than Pocket would ever have guessed. There were creeks and streams by some of the farms in Sail, but nothing like this.

"I could never skip stones all the way across," she said.

"I suppose not," Wick said.

"But how will we even cross?"

"I think I know a way," said a third voice. Both of the travelers turned at the sound of this very low, very deep, booming voice. There was a man walking towards them. This man was a tall man, nearly three times their height. He wore a long, dark coat with big silver buttons all down the front. His head was hidden away deep in a floppy hood.

"Who are you?" Wick asked.

"I am a fisherman," said the man.

"A fisherman?" Pocket asked. "Where is your fishing pole?"

"They are over there," The fisherman said, pointing off in towards the shore.

The Thornhaired Princess

Sure enough, when Pocket looked in that direction she saw a fishing pole. What's more is that she saw *three* fishing poles.

"Why on earth do you need three fishing poles?"

"Because," the fisherman said. "I have one for each pair of hands!" The long coat ruffled and flexed until six hands emerged from the coat's six sleeve holes.

"That is highly unusual," Wick said.

"A six-handed fisherman?" Pocket asked. "Who ever heard of such a thing?"

"Why me of course," said the fisherman. "For I am the six-handed fisherman."

"Well that's all well and good, and we're pleased to meet such an interesting person, but we are on a quest and if you have a way to get across the river we would be very happy to hear it."

"That's very simple my young friends. Up ahead along the shore you will find three boys with an amazing gift for building. They will build you a bridge to anywhere you wish to go."

"That is a nice talent," Pocket said.

"Indeed it is," said the fisherman. "But be warned, they will charge a fee for their service and sometimes it can be quite tricky."

"Hmm, well I appreciate the warning," Pocket said.

"Yes, thank you, sir," Wick added.

"No trouble at all. Have fun on your adventure," the fisherman called.

The two travelers left the fisherman to his fishing and continued upstream. As they walked through the grass and sand of the river's bank, up ahead large shapes came into view. Big gray blocks like shadows loomed far up ahead, maybe a mile or two or even farther than that.

"What is that big thing?" Pocket asked.

"That is Vent," Wick said.

"That? It's so big."

"It is quite big, maybe a dozen of our little Sails all in one."

Pocket couldn't imagine such a place as big as that. Maybe one day she could visit, once they finished with their quest.

Up ahead they spotted what could only be the camp of the three boys the fisherman spoke of. It was three miniature cabins, all made with strange angles and odd staircases and rope bridges leading to the others. Why they needed bridges between cabins on the ground, Pocket couldn't have guessed, but she like them all the same as they looked ever so fun.

They came to the cabins, but kept a distance before calling out.

"Hello there," Wick called.

"Well hello to you," a voice called. It was the same low, same deep voice from before. From behind the fisherman had followed them all the way.

"You again?" Pocket asked.

"Yes, of course. Who else would it be?"

"Why the three boys, of course, the ones you told us would be here."

"But they are! Just have a look."

The fisherman's jacket came unbuttoned revealing the secret. Out came three boys stacked on top of one another.

"I'm so glad I can see again," the middle one said. "That gets very difficult."

"You two need to get off now," said the bottom one. He was the stockiest and strongest of them all, clearly. Pocket briefly wondered whether he was the strongest because he carried the other two often or if he had to carry the other two because he was the strongest. Then she realized how silly this all was and forgot all about it.

"If you were *you* this whole time then why not just say so?" Pocket said.

"Because we like playing tricks!" the top one said. They had all climbed down now so really he wasn't the top anymore.

"You already know why we're here, of course," Wick said. "So would you mind taking us where we'd like to go?"

"We sure could," said the one who had been the middle.

The Thornhaired Princess

"But it will cost you," said the top.

"Yes, of course, we'd be happy to pay," Wick said. "Just tell us how much?"

"That depends on where you want to go," the top one said.

Pocket and Wick told the story of the theft of their tree and where they needed to get. They really only knew the sky island was somewhere off to the north. Practically everyone had heard that it made port at a place called the Stone Tower every so often. That was there best shot at getting up there, really the only one that they knew.

"Hmm, that is interesting," said the top boy. "Very interesting."

"That's a dangerous area. The Thornhaired Queen lives near there," said the middle boy.

"Yes, her realm covers most of the river and she is very protective of her lands," said the bottom boy.

"I thought you could take us anywhere?" Pocket asked.

"In a way," said the bottom boy. "But in another way we have to be able to get there in the first place."

"See we are bridge builders," said the middle point. "And to build a bridge to anywhere, you need a safe place to stop at each end."

"I see," Pocket said, though she was quite confused.

"Tell you what. We know a shortcut that might help you, and we can build a bridge to there." The top one was thinking hard as he said this. "But our price will be difficult."

"You are our only hope and a shortcut would be greatly appreciated," Wick said.

Pocket wasn't so sure, but these boys seemed quite helpful if a little silly, but they kept talking of tricks and that made her worry.

"Right then. There is a person up in Vent that makes costumes. Very special costumes. We would like three different animal costumes, one for each of us."

"Costumes?" Pocket asked.

"That is our price. Will you pay it?" said the top boy.

Pocket and Wick looked at each other. Wick could only shrug as he agreed, "We will, but it will take some time to get to Vent."

"Ah, but that's where you're wrong. See we can get to Vent easily and to show you that we are not lying about our talents, we will take you there free of charge." the middle boy said.

"Really?" Pocket asked.

"Of course!" the bottom boy said.

And with that Pocket and Wick witnessed the wonderful talent of the bridge builder brothers. The bottom boy stayed on shore holding on to two great iron bars stuck into the ground. The other two seemed to float on the air like hummingbirds. But they weren't really floating, Pocket could see, they were just moving ever so swiftly. The top boy seemed to dance across the water, laying out what appeared to be long, skinny pipes this way and that, creating a track as he went. The middle boy set up a small little cart with wheels on either side of great iron rails.

"Ready?" the middle boy asked.

Pocket and Wick looked to each other again and then back to the strong bottom boy. The great strong boy stood on the shore holding onto the tubing smiled at the travelers ever so broadly. Pocket offered her hand to the brother in the cart, who pulled her up and in with Wick following, climbing up behind. Once they were settled and buckled in place, the cart started moving and off shooting over water at a rapid pace, sped along by the middle brother's fast moving arms as he rowed and rowed the cart across the rails, chasing after his brother much quicker than snails.

Chapter 7

Vent

The cart zoomed and whirred all across the pipework laid out by the top brother.

"We are going quite fast now," Pocket said, not really talking to anyone.

"This is only half as fast as normal," said the middle brother. "But you guys seemed to have had a long day so we didn't want to scare you."

Pocket was ever so thankful that they were not going any faster. She wasn't quite sure she could handle any more speed with the cart's shifting and swaying. It felt as if the cart may tip and spill them in the river at any moment.

The cart began to slow until it came to a gentle rest. Pocket realized now she had closed her eyes so she opened them finding that they had stopped among the series of long wooden docks. The massive city of Vent loomed just beyond, its tall buildings and chimneys puffing with smoke.

"I am glad that is over," Wick said to the bridge builder boys. "But thanks for the ride all the same."

"You're quite welcome," the top brother said. He sat perched on the edge of their cart on the bridge made of rails. "Now if you will bring the costumes back here, we will take you to where you need to go."

Pocket and Wick started down the dock and off toward Vent. The buildings here seemed taller than the tallest in Sail. Every one of them felt grand and beautiful. Carved stones and beautiful clay tiled ceilings of red or brown or black lined every street. Shops with shoppers created a buzz around every corner.

"This place is quite large. How do you suppose we will find the costume maker?" Pocket asked.

"I don't know. I've only been here once and that was to sell candles to the book-makers."

"The book-makers?" Pocket said, quite curious. "That is something I'd like to see."

"We can go there if you like. It's the only place I know. Perhaps they'll be able to help us with where we should go."

They went down a few streets and alleys until Wick found his direction. He checked a few streets until he found the one he recognized. Together he and Pocket made their way through the busy city, with its smokestacks billowing and its chimneys puffing.

"Here we are!" Wick said, pointing at a sign overhead.

Pocket read, "The Pagemakers" on the large wooden marker. Quite an unusual name if she said so herself.

They stepped into the shop and found several people hard at work. Stacks of paper filled every table along with good leather bindings, ripe for new pages.

"Can we help you, young ones?" a man said, standing behind the counter. He had a mustache and glasses looking down at Pocket and Wick, eying them carefully. Nearby a young worker, maybe a year or two older than Wick looked at them curiously as well. This boy was wearing a thick wool hat indoors, which was most unusual of all. Pocket supposed they didn't get many visitors and bookmaking shop.

"We're looking for someone?" Wick said, suddenly unsure.

"Is that a question or is that what you're doing?" the man and the counter said.

"It's what we're doing," Pocket replied.

The Thornhaired Princess

"Ah, is that person a book-maker, then?"

"No, sir. We're looking for a costume maker," Wick said.

"I see. So why are you at a book-maker shop? You'll see no costumes here."

"This is the only place I know, sir," Wick said.

"Ah, yes. You have that out of town look about you now that I look at you both. Well, I'm afraid there are only book-makers here. A costume maker would seem to be in the clothing district, but then I've never heard of such a thing."

"Sorry to bother you then, sir," Wick said. He made as if to leave, but Pocket didn't budge. She'd been keeping an eye on the workers and it seemed quite odd. They were taking the pages from various tables, reading them, and then sticking those into new leather bindings.

"What exactly is it you do here?" Pocket asked. "This all seems very unusual."

"We are bookmakers," the man said, as if that covered it.

Pocket said nothing, looking at the man and waiting.

He shrugged. "The pages are written by various people and sent here. We take the pages and put them together in a way that makes sense. Is that really so unusual?"

"Yes!" Pocket said.

The man shrugged again. "That is what we do."

There was nothing for it. The two travelers left the bookmakers if for no other reason than to get away from the silliness.

"I'm sorry to say that was most odd," Pocket said.

"I agree," Wick said. "I never noticed what they were really doing there. It makes almost no sense at all."

"What should we do now?" Pocket asked. "Do you know where this clothing district might be?"

"I'm afraid not. But it is getting dark. Perhaps if we find an inn we can find both a place to stay for the night and directions for the clothing district."

Suddenly Pocket's feet seemed terribly sore and she could think of nothing better than a good rest. "That sounds like the most wonderful plan. You don't suppose those silly bookmakers would know of an inn."

"Maybe, but I'm afraid to ask. They'd probably just tell us we should sleep on a roof!"

They laughed as they headed off. An inn shouldn't be too hard to find, even in a big city like this. They all had a familiar look and familiar sounds, so far as they knew. They made slow and steady progress looking at the buildings trying to find one that looked right. But street after street they found nothing, no inns in sight.

"I'm getting a bit worried now," Pocket said.

"I'm sure an inn will turn up before long. So long as this silliest of cities actually has one!"

Continuing on, they stayed hopeful that the next building they check would be the last. They went into a little shop where the only person inside was an older little woman wearing a big fluffy sweater. She could have been either of their grandmothers.

"Excuse me," Wick said. "But could you point us towards an inn?"

"In, dear? You're already inside."

"I know that, ma'am. I'm looking for an *inn*, a place to stay for the night."

"Of course, dear, you can come in."

"Good gracious," Pocket said. "This whole city is upside down!"

They left the little shop more frustrated and troubled. But the sky was darkening quickly. They would want to get somewhere comfortable soon. More than anything it would be good to get off their feet.

They went back the way they had come thought they did not notice. One turn and then another and they were almost all the way back to the bookmakers' shop. They took a road to the north that would have led them back where they started when Pocket stopped altogether.

"I'm now fairly certain we are quite lost."

"Are we?" Wick asked.

"Yes you are," said a voice from behind. They turned and saw nothing but a shadow slide out from the corner.

"Who is there?" Pocket called.

"It's just me." A boy stepped from the alley. He wore a strange hat, one like a sock with a ball dangling off the back. "I'm sorry but I've been following you for a bit and I had to stop you from going in circles. I heard you back there and I think I can help you find what you're looking for."

"Great!" Wick said. "We could use help finding an inn as everyone in this city seems to have forgotten their own feet."

"No, not the inn." the boy said.

"Wait a minute," Pocket said, finally recognizing the hat. "You're one of those silly bookmakers."

"I don't know if we're all that silly," the boy said, "but you're quite right, I'm one of them."

"Oh no, not one of you," Wick said.

"I think that's uncalled for," the boy said. "I'm only trying to help."

"You're right," Wick said. "I apologize. I am just quite tired."

"No trouble at all," the boy said. "Now, how about we find you an inn, and we talk about how I can help you find the wonderful and colorful costume maker."

Chapter 8

Mittens

They took a few steps letting this mysterious boy lead the way. They headed towards a darkened street in the evening growing late. It all suddenly seemed very unusual. Pocket planted her feet so suddenly Wick almost tripped right over her.

"Why are we stopping so soon after starting?" Wick groaned.

"Just one second, stranger," Pocket said. "We were tricked once by a six-handed fisherman. How do we know you are not tricking us also?"

Wick gave her a look. He whispered, "But that worked out fine."

"Yes, but this place is strange enough and this boy worked in the strangest place of all," Pocket whispered back.

"That is very fair," said the stranger boy. "What is it you'd like to know?"

"Two things. First, we need your name. And Second, we need to know just how you might know this costume maker we seek."

The stranger looked thoughtful, looking over the two adventurers. "I think I can answer both of those quite easily. But you must make a promise. This promise is dear, one only a friend could make. After this we must be considered friends."

"If you don't mean to trick us," Pocket said. "I'm happy to be friends with you, strange boy."

The Thornhaired Princess

"Me too," added Wick.

"Good then." With a flourish the strange boy reached up to his unusual hat and pulled it off with a single tug. When the hat was off the boy changed to something else. The *he* became a *she* right before their eyes. But it was not just the face that shifted, it was everything. The clothes, even her shoes shifted. Pocket was amazed a little stocking cap could change so many things!

"Well you did trick us after all," Wick said.

"No, I'm sorry, it is not you I meant to trick but my boss and the others at the book-making shop." The girl tucked the hat into her coat and brought out a pair of mittens, which she slipped over her tiny hands.

"Why ever would you need to trick a book-maker?" Pocket asked. "Not that would blame you for doing so, of course."

"They only allow boys to work there and it has always been my dream. So I had the costume maker make me this hat to disguise me as a boy."

Pocket looked that stranger boy who was now a stranger girl. She was quite lovely with short red hair and surprising green eyes.

"So this is the promise you are asking for, isn't it? To keep your secret?"

The girl nodded.

"OK. That is easy enough. I don't think it's fair for you to have to disguise yourself, but if that is what you feel you must do then so be it."

"It is no big deal. I will be finishing my first book soon and when I'm done I'll show them what I am. They cannot get rid of me once I've proven I can do the job as well as they can."

Wick nodded thoughtfully. "If the hat is a costume like the bridge boys desire, it is clear you know the costume maker. But do you know how to find him again?"

"I do, but I will need a favor."

"A promise and a favor?" Pocket asked.

"Yes indeed. But first let us get you somewhere warm where

The Thornhaired Princess

you can eat and rest. The costume maker won't see anyone this late no matter how urgent your plight. Might as well be safe and sound for the night."

"That sounds good to me," Pocket said. "We can discuss over a nice meal."

So the girl led them to a lovely inn. It was not hard to see why they could not find an inn on their own. The one they found was much bigger than any back home. They would never have thought a building so large, with four floors and two sets of double doors, could be as cozy and warm as an inn. But cozy and warm it was, complete with a roaring fire and friendly face behind the bar.

The girl set them up with two rooms for which Pocket and Wick were happy to have. Along with the food they'd been given a small bag of coins for just such an occasion. They put their bags into their rooms and met once again in the common room on the main floor near the main entrance while the girl waited at a table.

"So you had a promise, so now what's the favor?" Wick said.

"The promise was to show you who I am. The favor is to get you there."

"You drive a hard price, strange girl. But go ahead and ask your favor," Wick said.

"I need to visit a special place, but it is in a dangerous part of town. You two are adventures, unless I miss my guess. If you will aid me in getting to where I would to go, I will happily return that favor and show you the way to your goal. Deal?"

"You have a deal on one condition," Pocket said.

"Fair enough," the girl asked.

Pocket gave her a grin. "We still don't know your name!"

"Oh! Of course. My name is Mittens and it is a pleasure to meet you both."

"Very well, Mittens. I am Pocket and this is Wick. We will happily go with you to where you'd like as long as the costume maker is our final stop. We are on an important journey."

"That much is obvious," Mittens said. "I will come back for you

The Thornhaired Princess

first thing in the morning. From there I will take you the edge of town where we will find the place I wish to go."

The innkeeper brought over three plates of warm food. Some turkey, some rolls, and a corner of steaming greens. They ate happily; glad to have something warm in their bellies.

"Do you care to tell us anything about this place you'll be taking us?" Wick asked.

"I dare not," Mittens said. "I would not want to fill your sleep with dreadful dreams."

Pocket and Wick looked to each other with eyes wide as saucers.

"Do not fret too much," Mittens added. "For in this scary place is a smaller, happier spot. I desire to visit a wishing well of an unusual sort. Perhaps you will be able to make wishes of your own."

"That doesn't sound so bad," Pocket said.

Mittens shrugged. "I should be off so you two can rest. We have a big day tomorrow."

"Good night, new friend," Pocket said.

With that Mittens left while Pocket and Wick went up to their rooms for a good night's rest. They drew warm baths and dressed in their pajamas and lay awake longer they both wished. Each had separate thoughts in their separate rooms, but both thought of wishes, and how they might come true.

Chapter 9

The Wishing Well

True to her word, Mittens came to the inn first thing the next morning. What Pocket never realized is that first thing in the morning, is very, *very* early.

"Rise and shine!" Mittens said, popping her head in the door of Pocket's room.

"What is going on?" Wick said from across the hall. His hair was messy and sideways as he peeked out from his room.

"It's time to go," Mittens said. "If we hurry we might see *them*."

"Them? Who is '*them*'?" Pocket crawled out of bed and changed out of her pajamas.

"Oh, the 'them' I'm talking about is a special group of my friends. They live out by the wishing well."

"If you have friends out by the wishing well, then why do you need us?" Wick asked. He came out of his room dressed and ready to go. He wore a hat similar to Mittens' covering his messy hair. That was good thinking, Pocket thought, so good in fact that she wished she had a hat as well now.

"Silly boy, these friends of mine only appear for a few hours and then they leave for the day. And they cannot go to the place beyond their homes, which is exactly where we need to go."

The three left the inn and let Mittens lead the way. She had a hop in her steps that hadn't been there yesterday. Pocket smiled as their new friend must really be excited about this wishing well.

They crossed through an empty marketplace and walked down several vacant alleys, clearly it was just so very early no one else was up and about. Pocket could almost picture the people bustling about, filling the streets and shops all day and all night. But here right now before the sun came up the only sound was their footsteps echoing off stony ground.

"It isn't much further," Mittens said. "And I think we'll be there just in time."

"That is very good," Wick said. "I would very much like to meet these friends."

They came to a very tall fence that opened at an even taller gate. The sign overhead was big as well with big letters. The sign read Cemetery of Vent, which gave Pocket pause.

"They should be just ahead," Mittens said, heading through the fence.

"I'm suddenly unsure of meeting these friends," Wick whispered to Pocket. "I'm not sure I want to meet people who spend time in a cemetery this early."

"I am, too, but a promise is a promise." Pocket went next and Wick followed him in.

The cemetery was large but actually quite pretty. It was all green grass with white or black stones marking each grave. This early in the day a nice layer of mist and fog settled upon the hills and down into valleys. It looked like little clouds had come down from the sky for a nice break in the morning grass.

"This isn't so bad," Pocket said. "It's a lovely cemetery."

"Maybe so," Wick said, but he looked off in the distance where Mittens had darted ahead. "But what are those?"

Mittens sat on a low stone wall. There on the other side were two figures all white and hazy much like the fog. Mittens turned and waved Pocket and Wick to come join her. As they drew nearer they saw that the figures Mittens was chatting with over the wall were not people at all.

"Why, you are ghosts!" Wick said.

"Indeed we are," said the taller ghost. This ghost appeared to be a man, if a ghost could be anything like that.

"You have ghost friends," Pocket said. "That is quite unusual."

"It is, I know," Mittens said. "But they are the ones who raised me. They died in a fire a couple of years ago. My brother and I made it out but, well, now he's gone too, now, gone somewhere far."

The other two ghosts looked sad for a moment as if deep in thought or trying to remember.

"Well we're pleased to meet you," Pocket said. "It's not every day we get to meet ghosts."

"In fact you're the very first," Wick said.

"That hardly seems fair," Mittens said. She didn't look so sad now.

"We understand you're going with our dear Mittens up to the well?" the shorter ghost offered. Pocket now saw that this ghost was in fact a lady ghost.

"We are," Pocket said. "I'm actually quite curious about it now."

"Don't let us keep you. Our time here is almost up anyway." The two ghosts looked to each other, then to Mittens.

"Goodbye my friends," Mitten said. "It was good to see you again."

"And you," the lady ghost offered.

The two ghosts drifted away, up and over to a pair of stones. They hovered there for a moment before vanishing in the light. There had been other ghosts flying around as well, those all *poofed* out of sight with the arrival of the morning sun.

"That was very interesting," Wick said.

"Thank you for letting us meet them," Pocket said.

Mittens only smiled. "Come on, the way is up ahead. We should get going."

They crossed the cemetery, walking on the smooth path that weaved through. They came to its end, but Mittens kept going into

The Thornhaired Princess

the grass. She went up the small stone steps that were cut into a hill. She marched with purpose while Pocket and Wick followed, trusting their new friend but they were nervous still.

The steps went up and around and down and through, all over a set of hills leading up through a tiny wooded glade. Finally, the steps ended and they came into a clearing. At its center was the little stone wishing well, covered by a little simple roof.

"That didn't seem very scary," Pocket said.

"No, not scary. But without someone with me I hardly ever find ways to leave the ghosts. I usually sit at their grave until one of the workers comes and gets me."

"Then I'm glad I'm here," Pocket said. "Since this is where you want to go."

"So how does this work, this wishing well?" Wick asked.

"It's another part of the danger. See to make the wishes work you have to offer different things for different wishes. Coins only bring luck, and small luck at that. To help a sick person you must give a drop of blood. To help a lost person find their way, or for you to find yours, you must give a cut of your hair, and to bring love and joy you offer something of your own."

"And you just drop it in?" Pocket asked.

"Drop it in and make a silent wish. That is all it takes for the well to cast its spell."

The three thought for a minute, but then Mittens stepped up to the well. "I will show you how. I always wish for the same thing." She reached into her coat and pulled out a pair of scissors. She leaned over the well and cut off a bit of her hair. Pocket then realized why her hair was so short. She must have come here often over the years.

Wick went next. He took the scissors but instead of hair he pricked his own finger sending a drop of blood into the well.

Pocket went last and also went slowest. There were so many things to wish for, how could she decide?

At last she made up her mind and reached into her bag. There wasn't much there but food and some clothes and the puppet of course. But there was one other thing, something very precious to her.

The nice writing pen that her father had given her. She didn't want to give it away now that she knew its roots, but maybe this was its purpose and there was a price to be paid for this wish. She threw it in the well this day, because luck was not needed.

"It is done," Mittens said. "Your wishes have been made. Now it is time to fulfill my end of the bargain."

"It is, but I want to thank you for bringing us here. This was a wonderful time," Pocket said.

"It truly was," Wick agreed.

"I'm glad you think so," Mittens said with a smile. "Now let us be gone from here. The costume maker waits!"

Chapter 10

The Costume Maker

It was not even yet noon as Mittens led Pocket and Wick to the costume maker. They were traveling back through the city the way they had come. They passed the inn then the book-makers shop then even the docks where they had arrived.

"If we were this close when we got here I will be most furious," Wick said, though he was laughing.

"Don't be so silly," Pocket said. "Surely we didn't pass it on the way in."

"I doubt it," Mittens said from ahead. "The costume maker lives quite far."

Their guide spoke the truth as they kept right on going. They went passed the docks and into a part of the city that felt older and, well, *thicker*. Here the buildings were all crooked and leaning and not it neat little rows. There were hardly any tall buildings here either, none over two stories. It reminded Pocket of home in a way, but in other ways it was nothing like Sail at all. Things were cramped and dirtier but also parts here and there felt both elegant and quaint. Some buildings were cracked, but those same cracks had been filled with dirt where flowers now sprouted. The people she saw were all smiley and hard at work, either in their yards or helping out in a neighbor's.

The Thornhaired Princess

"This is an interesting area," Pocket said.

"Oh, I'm glad you think so," Mittens said. They turned a corner and she pointed. "That's where I used to live before...well, you know."

The house she pointed to looked much newer than the others. Then Pocket realized she had said "used to live" and Pocket wondered. Pocket thought about what Mittens had said regarding her parents and the fire. This must have replaced her old house with this new one some time ago.

Mittens said no more about it and it was none of Pocket's business so she let it go. They continued on, making good pace through this little neighborhood. At last they came to the end of a row of houses where a building sat that was quite unusual indeed. She would have never thought to stop here had Mittens not done it for them. It looked plain enough, much like all the other little cottages. But something about it made her want to leave. It was like she couldn't quite look straight at it.

"Strange isn't it?" Mitten said.

"Quite strange indeed," Pocket said.

Wick simply looked away, as if ignoring the house all together.

Mittens shrugged. "He doesn't like visitors at his home."

"Will he be mad that we're here then?" Pocket asked. She dearly wanted this part of the quest to be over and to get the costumes and be on their way. Pocket didn't want to be here any longer than necessary, though she liked Mittens and was glad to have met her. Pocket made a mental note to tell Mittens that before they left her to continue their journey.

"No, I'm here with you so all should be," Mittens said.

She led the group up to the front door. Once they were on the porch the feeling went away. Wick waved a hand in front of his face as if trying to swat a bug.

"That's even stranger," he said.

"Oh yes," Mittens agreed. "We're inside the barrier now."

Pocket wondered at what kind of barrier needed to be on house

The Thornhaired Princess

as Mittens knocked on the door with the big brass handle and waited. Soon they heard footsteps approaching and at last a great eyeball appeared in the window.

"Who is out there on my porch?" said the Costume Maker. He had a nice voice, like that of a singer.

"It's me, Mittens."

"Mittens?"

"Yes, sir."

"Since when do you come in threes?"

"Since never, sir. I brought friends. They have a special task and wish to speak to you."

"I guess I couldn't say no to my dear Mittens. Well what are you waiting for, come in!"

"We're waiting for you to open the door, sir," Mittens said.

"Oh, of course you are!"

The Costume Maker swung open the door and waved the three kids inside.

The house was most unusual, that much was clear. Outfits and coats and shirts of all kinds were hanging from every hang-able place Pocket could see. There were tables and mannequins covered in costumes and cloth. But what was more is that the house seemed to just go on and on.

"How is this possible?" Wick asked, clearly thinking the same thing as Pocket.

"What do you mean?" the Costume Maker asked.

"This house is three -- no *four* -- times bigger on the inside than on the out!" Wick said.

"Well of course," the Costume Maker said. "I need more space in here than out there."

"But it is impossible," Pocket said. "Isn't it?"

"Not impossible with my costumes."

"The house is wearing a costume?" Wick asked, not believing the man, not for one second.

"You don't think houses can have costumes? Is it really that much stranger than a person wearing a mask?'

"Yes!" Pocket said. "It is very unusual."

Mittens had taken a seat on a long couch next to a heap of coats and pants. She sat smiling at her new friends, delighting in their confusion. The Costume Maker stood at a large desk off near a corner.

"Unusual it may be but certainly not impossible." He looked up at Pocket and came over next to her. He took out a measuring tape and started to take her sizes.

"What is it you're doing, sir?" she asked.

"Oh nothing, dear." He went on measuring.

Wick continued to look around, aghast.

"Ah," the costume maker said once he'd finished with his notes. "I will ask you then, young lady, is my house really that much more unusual than a girl who can grow things with a song."

Pocket opened her mouth, but could think of nothing to say.

The costume maker quickly took measure of Wick.

"And a boy who can draw with candle fire? That is not unusual?" the Costume Maker added.

"I suppose we are all a bit strange, aren't we?" Pocket said. She saw Mittens still smiling.

"Quite so," the Costume Maker said. "Now, what is it that I can do for you, friends of Mittens? Or should I just make wild and crazy guesses all afternoon?"

"That might be fun," Mittens said.

"Maybe," the Costume Maker said. "But these two have a look of purpose about them."

Pocket looked to Wick, who was already looking at her.

"We certainly have a purpose, good sir. We are need of three costumes, one each for three different boys. They wanted three costumes of three different animals, each one a different size."

"I see. Did they request any specific animals?"

"They did not," Pocket said.

"Well, I can certainly do that, but you will have to buy them."

The Thornhaired Princess

"We don't have a great deal of money, sir," Wick said. "Only enough for the inn and supplies we may need for our journey."

"It sounds to me like these costumes you desire are supplies for your journey," the Costume Maker said. "As if they were they key to the whole thing even starting at all."

Wick and Pocket looked to each other. But it was Mittens who hopped up from her seat and whispered something in the costume maker's ear.

"I see," the Costume Maker said when she backed away. "Mittens here said you have something quite unusual in your belongings. I am willing to trade for that item, if you are willing to part with it."

Pocket glanced into her bag, wondering what he could mean.

"You mean my candles?" Wick asked.

"No, not those," the Costume Maker said. "I wouldn't dream of asking you for those."

Pocket opened her bag and knew right away. "He means this," she said, pulling out the left behind puppet.

"I do, indeed," the Costume Maker said.

"But we will need this further down the road," Wick said.

"What good will it do if you never make it down that road? Surely you can find a replacement for whatever is you plan to do with this."

Pocket was torn. The puppet had been the whole key to their plan, the reason they had left Sail and their reason to believe they could somehow get the tree back. Now it was about to be lost before they'd even truly started.

"He may be right, Pocket. Maybe we'll find something else to trade. The people we're after are thieves after all. They may want something they couldn't just steal for themselves."

Pocket shrugged. "OK, we agree to your deal, good sir. You may have the puppet in exchange for the costumes."

"Very good!" the Costume Maker said. He hurried off to a distant corner of your house.

49

The Thornhaired Princess

"You made a good choice," Mittens said. "That puppet will lead to no good for you."

"How do you know?"

"I just do," she said, and left it at that.

The Costume Maker returned with a set of three costumes. A lion, a wolf, and a bear. One for each of the boys.

"I consider our trade complete, it has been a pleasure," the Costume Maker said.

"Thank you, good sir," Pocket said.

She tucked the costumes away in her bag and with that Mittens led them out of the Costume Maker's unusual house.

Chapter 11

Across the Great River

Mittens walked with Pocket and Wick down to the dock where they'd first arrived in the city. When she turned to say goodbye Pocket noticed a sour look on her new friend's face.

"Thank you for all your help," Pocket said. "It was very good meeting you."

"Yes, this has been fun," Mittens said, brightening a bit. "I'll be sad to see you go."

"You can come with us if you like," Pocket said. "We could always use more help on our journey."

"That's very kind of you," Mittens said. "But I'm afraid I have too much here to take care of. Soon I will have finished my book. But you both have given me strength to walk in tomorrow, without my costume on and let them know who I really am."

"That is great news," Pocket said.

Mittens had a shy look about her suddenly. "I don't suppose," she said. "That you could tell me where you're going?"

"Of course we can!" Pocket said. "We are off to the sky island to get back something those puppets stole."

"Really? I almost wish I could go now. That sounds exciting."

"I hope it is that," Wick said. "But I think it's just going to be trouble."

"Well don't worry too much," Mittens said, brightening. "I'm on your side now so I will say wishes for you every day for you to have good luck."

"That is very kind," Pocket said. "But since we're going to the sky island maybe you could make a wish for something to catch us if we fall!"

"I can do that, too," Mittens said. "Wishes never run out as far as I know."

The new friends shared a laugh and an embraced just as the top bridge boy came strolling up the dock.

"Hello there," the bridge boy said. "Do you have the costumes?"

Mittens left them and headed back into the city. Pocket watched her go, sad to be minus a friend for their journey. Perhaps they'd see each other again, but perhaps not. Either way, she was glad they had met.

"Of course we have the costumes," Wick said to the bridge boy. "All three in fact."

They pulled the costumes from their bags and showed them to the boy. The lion, the wolf, and the bear all lay spread out for the top boy to see.

"These will do splendid!" he said. "Well, I suppose we must be off then."

"That is good to hear," Wick offered.

They all climbed into the cart as the top boy and the top boy built the new track of pipe.

"Does he already know where we're going?" Pocket asked.

The middle boy shook his head. "We must always start at our base. That is where our brother, the big guy, keeps things grounded."

Pocket leaned back in the cart as they sped off away from Vent. It was a lovely place and she'd love to come back.

They arrived back at the bridge boys' camp, all three of the boys looked very tired.

"I don't think you'll be able to get out right away," the big boy

The Thornhaired Princess

said. "It's been a long day already and it's barely the afternoon."

Pocket looked at the sky. The sun was still high overhead, but the boys looked quite sweaty and unkempt, even for them.

"Have you had a busy day?"

"Quite busy," said the middle boy. He was the most orderly of the three, but even he looked like he could use a good nap.

"Lots of early travelers up and about," the top one said.

"That reminds me," Wick said. "How did you know we'd be ready?"

"We just do," the top boy said, with a grin. "To be as successful as we are with bridges you have to know when people are in need of a crossing."

Wick supposed that was true. There seemed to be a great many magics in the world. Perhaps this was just another.

"So what do we do until we continue?" Pocket asked.

"Just have a rest and we'll make you a meal," the middle one said. He already had out a pot and pan heating it over a fire. It looked like had some rabbit and fish, which looked quite tasty.

She and Wick made themselves comfortable as the boys took their break. In truth she didn't mind waiting so much. They'd had a busy day as well and a busy night before. It was good to sit amongst friends especially on such a pleasant day.

They shared the rabbit and fish while Pocket offered up some nuts and fruit from home. It was a lovely meal and the boys were good company. When they'd finished they looked quite refreshed.

"What will you do with those costumes?" she asked.

"Why wear them of course," the middle boy said.

"But I mean why? For what purpose?"

"Same purpose as anything else. To have fun and enjoy them!" the top boy said.

Pocket shook her head but said nothing further. To think they'd got those costumes just for these boys to be silly would make her silly as well. But then she had met Mittens and that had been quite worth it.

The Thornhaired Princess

The boys all looked to each other, each giving a nod.

"We're ready to take you beyond the river," the big boy said. "Are you ready to go?"

"Quite ready," Wick said, and Pocket agreed.

They loaded into the cart once more and the top boy sped out laying the track across the water. They cruised along a bit faster this time. Pocket didn't mind so much now. The speed was intense, but not as bad as before. In fact, that wind in her face over the cool river felt quite nice.

A large shape emerged off in the distance. It was green and dark and loomed over the water.

"What is that?" Pocket asked.

"That is the Thornwood," the middle boy said. "The home of the evil queen."

"An evil queen?"

"Oh yes, quite evil. She has wrapped all the trees with thorny vines that grow from the hair on her head. They say she's attached to every plant in the forest, everything living and dead."

"That is quite a story," Pocket said. "Have you seen her?"

"Oh no, if I'd ever seen her, you would not be seeing me that much is the truth. They say anyone that goes in gets trapped there forever."

"Then why is it that we seem to be heading that direction?" Wick asked.

It was quite true that the path the top boy laid out seemed to be going straight for the forest.

"Just a short cut, my friends," the middle boy said. "No need to worry at all."

The cruised and they cruised continuing on their path across the river. Soon the other bank came into view. There was a large open plain spreading off towards the hills and mountains beyond. Those were nothing but dark shapes near the horizon. Another large shadow was also in view, that of the great sky island far and high up ahead, floating up there like a second moon. But it hung straight

The Thornhaired Princess

over the forest, though much further away. Pocket started to get a very bad feeling about the rest of the day.

They headed south and the Thornwood grew closer and closer, racing towards them in a wild hurry. It was clear now the stories had not been lies. Pocket could see the thorns twisting and encircling the trunks of the trees.

"That is quite a menacing place," she said.

The cart came to a sudden halt and sped sideways right towards the bank. It continued this way until it was over dry land, then it dumped out the travelers onto the sand.

"What is the meaning of this?" Wick demanded.

"You silly travelers, no one goes to the Sky Island by bridge. You must go up the Stone Tower which is sits deep in the forest where even we dare not go. This is as far as we go, to the edge of the wood. The shortcut is through there, if you only dare."

"This is a nasty trick," Pocket said.

"A trick, maybe, but it is not a lie. If you can make it through you will get to the place you wish to find."

"But what of the queen and all of these thorns?" Pocket said.

"Those are not our troubles," the middle boy said. "But I think two travelers like you may be beneath her notice. Just beware of all things, for there are creatures found inside worse than trees covered in thorns."

The boys took the bridge and sped away like the evil, tricky things they were.

"This is most troubling," Wick said.

"It is indeed," Pocket said. "But we are here now and this is all we can do. Maybe this Thornwood will prove less frightening than those boys make it sound."

"Let's hope," Wick said.

With uncertain strides the travelers marched forward, crossing into the forest covered in thorns.

Chapter 12

The Thornwood

"I must say this is as bad as I could imagine," Pocket said.

They kept close as they made their way into the Thornwood. The thorns were everywhere, covering every inch of the trees and the ground except for a narrow pathway barely big enough for both walking side by side. Even worse (if such a thing was possible) was that as soon as they took a few steps, the pathway shifted and turned direction as if someone was intentionally trying to confuse them...or leading them somewhere.

When Pocket had a second to think she thought of those tricky bridge boys and their talk of this evil queen. Maybe someone was tricking them with this ever shifting and silly path!

"This is not great," Wick said. "I have to admit."

They continued on, careful not to touch any thorns. They were thankful when at last they entered was seemed to be a clearing where the thorns thinned out and they could actually see the ground.

"This is much better," Wick said. "My feet finally have room to breathe."

"Yes it is, but we need to keep up our guard. Who knows what might be out in this crazy forest?"

They headed across the clearing glad to be away from the thorn-covered trees. A small lovely pond sat near the center. They went

The Thornhaired Princess

around it the south though Pocket stopped briefly to look into the water. It was crystal clear with a few fish dashing about.

"What is that lovely sound?" Wick said.

Pocket looked up and around. "I don't hear anything."

"You're missing out. It's the loveliest of songs."

"What are you going on about?" Pocket asked. "There's no music in this forest."

Wick wandered away from the pond off towards the tree line on the far side.

"Where are you going?" Pocket called.

"I must find it. The source of this lovely song must be quite lovely indeed."

"Well, wait for me!" Pocked dashed to catch up, but Wick kept going on ahead, ignored her entirely. She had nearly caught up when something leaped from the trees surprising her so she slipped and fell, scraping her knees.

Four figures, all appearing to be boys but also not boys at all. They were children made completely out of sticks. They had wood covered legs and wood covered arms. Hands and feet looked like a bundle of twigs. Even their heads and bodies appeared to be short, stubby logs. One of these unusual figures carried a flute that it seemed to be playing but Pocket could not hear any tune.

"Wick!" she shouted, trying to catch his attention.

But it was too late indeed. One of the figures scooped Wick up and carried him off deeper into the forest. A single stick kid remained, the tallest of them, the one carrying the flute.

"This way is not for you, little girl," he said. "Don't worry about your friend, he'll fit right in once he changes to lumber."

He played a quick tune that she still couldn't hear. And with that he too dashed off through the trees like a breeze through the leaves.

"Wick!" Pocket shouted again, but nothing could be done. The stick boys had him now, and now she was alone in this strange forest.

She went ahead, following the path that had led to Wick's

capture. She could think of nothing better to do.

"That silly boy, listening to silly songs I can't even hear. Boys! They're simply nothing but trouble."

Despite her anger and sadness, she just kept going. Maybe she would find him or maybe those stick kids would take her too. At least she would not be alone in this place. She marched on once again keeping watch for the dangerous thorns. Though it was easier now not having to make space on the path for anyone else.

That just made her sad all over. She wanted Wick back and even Mittens to be there. No one should have to go all alone on dark paths like these.

She walked and she walked until she heard a new sound. She stopped cold and focused on the noise. It was like a slithering, or a whipping, the sound of a snake through some weeds.

"Who is out there trying to frighten me?" she called.

Nothing answered.

She was stuck in the woods. Not wanting to run away, not wanting to stay. There was something out there among the dark trees.

From the shadows they came, new figures this time. The stick kids were gone, replaced by even creepier things. Large bug-like creatures, all made of twine. They were long and skinny and moved like willow vines.

"What are you, you silly things? Leave me at once!" Pocket tried to sound fierce, but her voice cracked likes trees in a storm. She was about to get dragged off, too, off somewhere worse like Wick and all alone too.

Two creatures became three, another coming from the trees. These *roplings* were quick and dashed around surrounding her path, blocking the way in and the way out.

She stood as firm as she could, but she was truly scared now. These things were quite big and she was so small.

Then came a third thing but different than all she'd seen. This shape moved quick like lightning through the trees. It crashed

"You're one of us now," the flute player said. "Now show us what gifts we can have."

Without asking or waiting for a reply, the stick kids grabbed Wick's backpack and started to root through it. They laughed and laughed as they flung the food he had brought down to the ground. But then they found something else and shouted with glee.

"What are these, new friend?" the flute player asked. He held up the candles and Wick let out a gasp.

"Do not touch those they are mine not yours. You are fiends most certainly, not friends at all."

"These candles are ours now, silly child. Now tell us, what do they do?"

* * *

"My name is Pocket," Pocket said to the thornhaired girl. "What is yours?"

"My name?"

"Yes, your name. It's kind of like what you are."

The girl was quiet for a moment. Thoughtful. "So you are a pocket?"

"No, that's my name. I guess a name is more like what friends and people call me."

The girl thought for a moment, looking off into the wood. "I am just me."

Pocket groaned but thought it best not to push it. The girl had saved her after all, no reason to be silly about it.

They walked together through the forest. As they traveled Pocket watched the girl carefully. More importantly she watched the forest *around* the girl. It was quite unusual, the way plants behaved. The thorny vines seemed to simply get out of the girl's way. She could walk where she pleased and her path remained clean. This place was truly her home in every way that could mean.

"So why are you in my forest?" the girl asked. Her voice sounded strange to Pocket. Her questions ended like questions, but not in the normal way. The girl seemed genuinely baffled that anyone was even talking to her at all. It was all very unusual.

"My friend and I are on a mission to the help our town, but now he's lost."

"Yes, I know. The stick ones have him."

"Is that truly as bad as I think it might be?" Pocket asked, voice very sad.

The girl hesitated. "Maybe."

They walked a bit further when the girl turned sharply. She raced off down the path before suddenly stopping and kneeling. Pocket raced to catch up to her, curious at what the girl could have seen from so far away and not at all curious to learn what might happen if she lingered behind, the thorny bushes may push in all around her, leaving her entwined.

The girl knelt over a small broken tree. It was a sprout no taller than her knee. But the girl seemed stricken and at a loss for what to do.

"Here, let me try," Pocket said.

The girl looked confused, but gave Pocket some room. Pocket knelt down beside her and dug a hole the size of her thumb. She replanted the roots and covered them with dirt. She sang the song of growing then stood up to wait.

The girl was looking at her most curiously now, almost as if afraid, but clearly not. It was a startled look but Pocket didn't fret, she just hoped her song would work here in the forest for her garden back home this place was not.

The little baby tree stood up straighter. Its broken part was healed now and it would grow like normal.

"Why did you do that?" the girl said with a whisper.

"I thought that's what you wanted," Pocket said, now scared she'd done something wrong.

"It was," the girl said. "But why did you do it?"

"You were upset, and I thought this would make you happy."

"It does," the girl said. "But why did you do it?"

"Because," Pocket said frustrated as could imagine. This girl seemed to be confused as if Pocket had baked a cake made of rocks. "We're *friends.*"

The girl stood quickly and gave a quick nod. "We must hurry now."

"Good, I would like to get moving again."

They ran and they ran, laughing like children, which they were, in a way, so they ran even more. Then finally they slowed when the forest got thick.

"Are we close to finding my friend Wick?"

"That's not where we're going. I cannot find them just yet."

"Then where are you taking me?" Pocket asked.

"To see my mother."

"Your moth--"

Pocket looked ahead and realized what she was seeing. The forest was not as thick as she thought for it was not the forest at all that stood just ahead. A single, massive tree, bigger than any two houses back in Sail, loomed ahead shadowing everything in its path. As they neared she saw it was not just a tree, but a tree palace at the end of this trail. Things became clear now as they stood outside, but Pocket wouldn't and couldn't believe what she knew was true.

"And who might your mother be?" she asked.

The girl cocked her head as she often had in their talking. "I am the Thornhaired Princess, friend Pocket. Surely you know that means my mother is the queen."

Chapter 14

The Queen

"The queen, you say?" Pocket asked. Her stomach felt queasy quite suddenly.

"Yes, of course."

They approached the giant tree, a massive nest of vines and twisted branches looming up ahead, surrounding everything in sight. Limbs stretched out like a storm clouds, seemingly forever, creating a canopy almost as big as the entire village of Sail. Pocket went as slow as she could manage. They made it to the base of the vine-covered stairs before a figure emerged from the shadowy doorway.

She was tall and magnificent, dressed head to toe in beautiful green clothes. Like the princess she had lovely purple eyes, though hers were deeper and darker, the color of the midnight sky. Her hair had thorns, though many more than her daughter. And her hair was different, too, thicker, and firmer, more like true branches of trees than strands of delicate hair.

"Hello, mother, I found someone near the forest door."

"Hmm," said the queen. Her voice, even with just an "hmm" was deep and resonant like the rumbling of thunder.

"Why are you here, girl? Why have you come to our home?"

"Mother, wait!" The princess ran up the stairs to her mother's side. She whispered something to the great queen who listened with eyes locked on Pocket. When the princess had finished the queen nodded just once.

"Show me," the queen said, but said only that.

Pocket stood silent and still and very confused. There were so many things she could show, but what did she mean?

It was then that the princess tossed something down; through the air it flew and landed on the ground. Pocket scooped it up and it all became clear. The queen wanted her to grow something, so grow something she would.

She planted the object the princess had thrown. It was a small pebble of white and perfectly round smooth stone. She dug a hole as deep as her hand, covered the stone with dirt and then she sang the song and waited for it to work.

The two girls and the queen waited as the sprout came up through the soil, a small white shoot hard and white and made of stone, with little stone pebbles dangling from its limbs all white and small and perfectly round.

"Hmm," the queen said again. "It has been a long time since I've seen a Grower from beyond my own borders."

"My father taught me," Pocket said. "And I think my mother was one as well."

"Was?" The princess asked.

"My mother passed away when I was born," Pocket said.

The princess turned to her mother and looked very confused.

"It is ok, daughter," the queen said, eyes still on Pocket. "I'm not going anywhere just yet."

The princess smiled then bounced down the stairs. She came next to Pocket once more and stood tall and proud. "She is my friend, mother. She and her friend need help."

"Friend you say?" the queen said. She sounded quite curious, Pocket thought.

The Thornhaired Princess

"I consider her a friend," Pocket said. "And she's right, my friend is quite lost."

The queen held Pocket in her gaze for a very long time, glaring into her eyes, straight through to her head. The queen's eyes were sharp, piercing, looking Pocket like she was a story to be read.

"I think I know what this is about," the queen said. "You are the one that planted the blue tree found in the village of Sail."

Pocket opened her mouth in surprise. "How did you know?"

"There isn't a thing grown in this world that I do not know of, child. But tell me, what do you know of me?"

"Umm," Pocket said. She didn't know quite what to say. Of course all she had known before today was that this queen lived here and that she was quite evil. "Well...I'm afraid I know very little, lady queen, and what little I've heard is only that you are mean."

The princess looked at her with a deep seeded frown. The queen held up a hand, calming the princess down.

"And what do you think now?" the queen asked.

"I'm not really sure," Pocket said honestly. "I know your daughter rescued me from some ropling beasts and that she might be a bit lonely. All these thorns all over the forest are not very inviting, yet once I've been through the forest with her, and at the doorstep of your palace, I can see that the Thornwood is quite lovely and nice."

"I see," the queen said. "That was very truthful, especially from one from the outside. Tell me good child, why have you come to my home?"

Pocket relayed the story of the theft of here tree and quest she'd set upon. They she talked about the town of Vent, Mittens, and the wishing well. Beyond that she talked of the bridge boys and their nasty trick, leaving them alone and with nowhere to go but into the wood and finally she ended with how she lost Wick.

"That is where you have been, I have no doubt, and why you came in is reasonable I can see. But why are you traveling at all, what is it you *want?*"

"First I need help getting my friend back. He was taken by creatures made of sticks."

"That could be tricky, though the stick boys are foolish. Eventually the will do something that will lead us to where they have taken your friend."

"That is good to know," Pocket said. "But we seek passage beyond the forest as well, to the Stone Tower. We are going to the sky island to recover our treasure."

The princess and queen suddenly snapped to attention. Both their gazes whipped from Pocket to somewhere far off, somewhere deeper into the forest.

"What is it? What's wrong?" Pocket asked.

"There is a fire," the queen said. "In the bog. I knew I was right but I didn't know I'd be proved right so quickly. The bog is where they have gone, no doubt that's where your friend will be."

The princess turned to her mother with narrowed eyes and a grin.

"Go, my daughter. Go and run. Find the fire and the other. I will stay here and talk with your…friend."

"I would like to go to. Wick may not trust the princess without knowing I'm safe here with you."

"I'm afraid this is my daughter's duty to do," the queen said. "Besides she's much faster than you."

The princess ran off, quickly as a cat. She raced through the thorns, her thorny hair trailing in the wind.

"I will help you, young child who can Grow, but I will need some things from you in return."

"Of course, of course, everything has a price."

"Is that what you consider my daughter's friendship? A price to be paid?"

"What? No! I merely expected the price to be some favor or task. Friendship is friendship, nothing more and certainly nothing less."

"I'm glad you think so, and you are right on both counts. I do have a favor to ask. A couple in fact. Come and walk with me, child, I have something to show you and a story to tell. My daughter will be fine and will return very soon. But while she's gone, you and I must discuss the moon."

Chapter 15

The Moon of Shifting Colors

Wick watched aghast as the stick kids pulled almost every candle from his bag. They stood them up lining them in crooked rows.

"What are you doing, you silly creatures?"

"We're making a fire!" they called.

"You can't do that! You don't know what you're doing!"

"Silence!" one of the kids roared. The stickling that had been playing the flute bent over the candles. He lit a fire from somewhere and somehow Wick couldn't see. They lit the candles and shouted in triumph and glee.

"Why would you want to start a fire in your home?" Wick asked, stunned and surprised.

The flute player whirled on him. "To hurt the queen and her daughter and make our home bigger, of course. Now out of the way, little one."

Wick stepped back away from the fire, back away towards a house among the trees and vines. His mother had explained how these new candles worked and wanted no part of the show that would follow. He'd nearly reached one of the tree-houses when a white candle ignited. The flare went up, exploding with light and showering the area in sparks. The stick kids covered their wood faces with wood arms and hands.

The fire from the candles grew and grew. It caught the vine ropes supporting the bridge and soon burnt right through. Luckily Wick had found solid ground. The platforms for the houses were strong hard wood that was reluctant to burn, but he was still high above ground.

"What now?" he asked aloud. The fire raged on, spreading throughout the bog.

A figure raced in, not like the stick kids at all. It brought with it a great wind and a wave called up from the wet land all around.

This figure swept away all the stick kids with a wave of its hand. It came to a stop down below, stocking-footed on a small patch of land. It looked up to Wick and waved him to come down. The figure was a she, with thorn-covered hair and a lovely green gown.

"Come down from there, boy named Wick. I have your friend Pocket safe and sound back in my home."

"How?" Wick asked, both regarding Pocket and the way to get down.

The girl looked around and dashed across the bog, searching for something Wick could not fathom. At last she stopped just below the house where he stood, she put her hand on the tree and that tree sank deep into the mud. When it stopped it put Wick eye to eye with the girl, making him so thankful he almost hugged her.

"Thank you, kind girl," Wick said. "I thought I was doomed."

"Gather your things. We must be free from here soon."

Wick did as instructed and picked up his bag. Luckily it was still intact with a number of candles still lying around. He picked those up and packed them away. They left the bog burning a bit, but the girl seemed unconcerned.

"It will burn out on its own and fuel some new growth," the girl said.

"That is good to know," Wick said. "Those stick kids are nothing but trouble."

The Thornhaired Princess

"You are not the first to be caught by their song. How do you think they keep growing in number with only boys in their gang?"

The princess and Wick ran together to get away from the bog. Once clear of that they slowed to a walk. They chatted a bit, mostly about Pocket, Wick wondering where she was also somewhere alone.

"Of course not, good Wick, she is with my mother the queen."

"Oh," Wick said, not sure if that was good. But this girl had saved him and apparently Pocket as well. Maybe the stories of the evil queen were just lies, lies like the bridge boys seemingly could not wait to tell.

* * *

Pocket walked with the queen through a moonlit glade. There were no thorns here to be seen save for those in the queen's hair.

"This is quite lovely, though why is the moon an unusual color?"

The moon was indeed a color not normal. It hung in the sky a pale green ball, the same as the princess's lovely old dress.

"That is what I came to show you, as the moon is different here in my Thornwood. It changes color based on the seasons and the mood of a strange creature far away."

"What kind of creature controls the moon?" Pocked asked.

"Why a moon creature, of course," the queen said.

"Oh, quite right," Pocket replied.

The moon is tied to the Thornwood in ways different than the rest of the world. The way it tugs at the oceans and other great bodies of water, the moon also pulls on us here, especially my daughter."

"The princess is tied to the moon in some unusual way?" Pocket asked.

"She is now and she will be. See, soon the moon will change color again, change just for my daughter. How these changes affect her depends on some rather strange factors."

The Thornhaired Princess

"I'm happy to help your daughter, the princess since she is my friend. What is it you would like or need me to do?"

"There is a place to the south of my palace, a small town hidden away in a fog. This place is called Silence by the people who stay there. They are good folk, not unlike you."

"A village?" Immediately she had thoughts of home but ignored them. "What will I find in this place?"

"Just the people, though I guess you never know. It depends on what you want when looking high and low. They are people that came here and never left. Their reasons are their own, but they are welcome as long as they're kind to my land and the things living within. If you help me in this task you may get a second gift that you did not intend."

"And this will help your daughter with the moon trouble?"

"No, that is a second part of the mission. In Silence you will find help and a guide for what I need. There is a place I cannot go, a valley of quiet and great power. It is there, in the Whistling Valley, you will find, if your ears are keen, a song I need to help my daughter grow in power and knowledge. It is these she will need so she may one day be queen."

"What kind of song could do all that?" Pocket wondered.

"Much like your song of growing, we have a song as well. It is a strange song, an ever changing tune, taught by the most ancient of living things."

"So I must retrieve this song from the valley and you'll help us get to the stone tower. That sounds like a fair deal."

"That is part one of our bargain, the other is a bit trickier and will cost me something as well."

"A cost from me that costs you as well that sounds almost frightening, my queen."

"In a way it is, but maybe it's nothing. My second need from you is the truth regarding my daughter."

"The truth? What truth don't you already know?"

"Your words of friendship, I must have them proven."

"That should be simple, your daughter is a lovely and amazing person."

"Amazing she may be, but her life is not now, nor will ever be easy. When you complete your mission I'd ask you to return and be a friend in truth, not one just passing on your journey."

"That is a fair request and a cost I will be glad to pay."

"That is most wonderful to hear," the queen said, offering Pocket a smile. "We should head back. Your friend is growing near."

They went back to the palace steps and stood waiting once more. Soon the princess and Wick arrived panting and tired but in danger no more.

"Pocket!" Wick shouted.

"Dear, Wick," Pocket said, throwing her arms around him. "I thought maybe you were lost forever."

"I did, too, but then this lovely girl here rescued me from those horrible creatures."

"She rescued me, too," Pocket said. "She's really quite something."

The princess looked away as she shuffled her feet. Pocket realized the then that the princess, this great and wonderful girl was quite embarrassed at the compliments of her daring feat.

"Daughter you have one more mission before we go to our rest for the day. These kids are heading to Silence, and you need to show them the way. Take them to the stream and give them passage across, explain how to find the Guides by using light of a certain color."

"Of course, mother, but must they leave so quickly." The princess sounded sad and suddenly very lonely.

"I'm afraid so dear, but they will return soon enough." The queen eyed Pocket.

"We will indeed," Pocket said. "We will visit once we retrieve our treasure."

"We will?" Wick asked, looking around the Thornwood.

The Thornhaired Princess

"Of course, silly Wick," Pocket said. "We have friends here now, ones we should see over and over."

The princess frowned ever so slightly, but waved them to follow.

"This way my...friends." She offered a slight smile. "The sooner you're off the sooner we meet once again!"

They were on their way all over again, through the trees and darkening sun overhead. Pocket smiled to her friend Wick as they followed their new friend off through the thicket and brush, this mysterious girl with the thorns on her head.

Chapter 16

The Road to Silence

The princess led them through the forest. They went over small hills and large pretty gardens. The stream just ahead was a sight to behold. A small line of bluish-green cut through the thorny brush, flowers, and ground so rocky, ancient and old.

The princess went up to the edge of the stream and raised a hand. She spoke some words Pocket could not understand. A large tangle of vines shot up from the ground, crossing the rushing water to other side safe and sound.

"Here is where you will cross and return when you're done doing whatever my mother has asked. Head that direction until you find the Great Hands. There you will find the Guides, or really they will find you. They are a quiet lot, but they will come to answer the call of a bright purple light. There is a flower found beyond the stream you can burn to create this color. Wick, I believe you can take care of the rest?"

"I can indeed, fair princess." Wick said.

"Very well. See you when you have recovered your tree," the princess said. She stepped out of the way as the two travelers crossed her sturdy bridge.

"This is much better way of crossing than that silly cart of the bridge boys," Pocket offered.

The Thornhaired Princess

The princess smiled and waved as they left. She turned away with a tear in her eye, confused at where it had come from as the only drops of water she knew came from the sky.

The princess went home, back to palace. The travelers crossed the bridge and deeper into the forest.

"Will we really see her again?" Wick asked.

"I hope so," Pocket said, for more reasons than one.

Pocket and Wick headed through the forest. The thorny vines behaved differently now. They kept out of their way giving a wide path for the princess's new friends to travel upon. Together they continued through the forest making good pace, only stopping once to grab a quick snack before resuming their quest.

An hour or so later they came upon two giant stone stumps. They sat side by side, a perfect pair, but of what they couldn't say. Wick passed between them and turned around for a better view. With a great wide smile, he waved Pocket through.

"We've found them," he called. "These are not just silly stumps, but the Great Hands that must have once held something truly quite large."

Pocket came with and looked at the hands. They were big indeed and it seemed Wick was right, they had once held something up, for the palms were outstretched as if giving a push.

"I wonder what was here, so long ago," Pocked said.

"That's something only the queen may know," Wick asked. "But for now we must leave that alone."

Pocket searched the ground until finding the small purple flower. She plucked a couple and gave them to Wick. He lit one of his candles and set the flower in to be greeted by a great burst of purple light and sparks making a shower. They continued down the path guiding their feet, waiting and hoping to find who they were supposed to meet.

Not long after lighting the candle a figure emerged, from where or how, neither child could say. Suddenly the person was there, wearing a long black robe, with hair brown like the wood. The travelers stopped and let this new person approach, drawn to their purple flame as the princess had promised.

"Hello, travelers," the robed man said, his voice wispy like tall grass. "What can we, the Quiet Ones, do for you?"

"The Quiet Ones?" Pocket asked.

"Of course, we come from Silence so we are called the Quiet Ones."

"I see. Well, we were sent by the queen to find your village. She taught us about the flame and finding you."

"That is most grand," said the robed Quiet One. "But what is it the queen wants that she sent the two of you?"

"Um," Pocket said, unsure what to reveal. The truth was always best she thought so went on ahead. "We are to find the Whistling Valley. We are to retrieve the song."

The robed man looked up, high to the sky. "Ah yes, the moon changes," he said. "Come, I will take you to my home."

The robed man showed them the way, walking smoothly through the Thornwood as if walking on a nice rug. He led them to the edge of a cliff. Off to one side sat a set of steps leading down. Wick saw that beyond the drop was nothing but fog, impossible to see through, just like that bog.

"You must put out your flame now, good traveler for the fog dislikes fire and light."

Pocket looked down over the edge. "But how do we see without our way being clear?"

"You just have to trust that you will know the way. But worry not, for the queen sent you. All will be well or else she would not have told you of this place."

Pocket wasn't so sure, but Wick strode right up. With a step down the stair he simply vanished from sight.

With a groan Pocket followed, stepping up to edge. She waited a moment, catching her breath. The step was ever so small but it felt forever long. Over she went with that small little step, away from what she could see and down into the fog.

The Thornhaired Princess

The fog was cool, but dry and quite pleasant. It was impossible to see where to go, so only tiny steps forward she went. Step after step she made her way through. Always going down, she felt, but never turning at all. With a step like the rest she burst from the fog, standing before was the town, Wick, and the robed man all.

"Well, we made it through," Wick said.

"Yes, that was actually quite easy," Pocket said.

"I told you there was nothing to fear. Now come along, I will show you the wonderful village we have built here."

The town of Silence was unusual to say the least. It had no buildings that were proper, all of them with wheels and hitches but no animals of which to speak. All their homes were all great wagons sitting in place, but judging by the tracks through the dirt even with no animals to pull them anywhere in sight, the entire village was mobile come day or night.

The robed man led through all, pointing out the homes of the doctor, the wagon drivers, the food gatherers of which there were four. He even pointed out which wagon belonged to the candlemaker which made Wick smile even more.

There were other reminders of Sail here as well. Though their houses could roll, the town was lovely all the same.

"This place is quite nice," Pocket said. "But how do you move without horses?"

"Ah, that is our trick," the robed man said. "For we are builders and makers of machines that move with pushes instead of pulls. They're powered from within by special things, items of metal and fire, powered by springs."

"I'd like to see that," Wick said.

"Perhaps you will, but now we need to find what you seek. You need a guide to the valley and that means you need a sneak."

"A sneak?" Pocked asked. "What kind of valley requires a sneak to get in?"

"The Whispering Valley," the robed man said. "It requires stealth and secrecy for the builders of the monument you hunt are quite big and scary, but also slow and unsteady."

The robed man gathered the people of the town and the center of the wagons. There were a large number of people, more than in Sail. Pocket saw right away why this place was secret. Everyone here was smiling and happy and safe all the same. This is what the queen wanted her to see, she realized just then. There is safety in the Thornwood, the scary stories are only told by fools who knew nothing. These people were hidden just fine in their fog, but from the outside world and the sky island puppets, the queen protected them all.

When everyone had gathered the robed man made his announcement. "These young travelers seek the valley as a favor to the queen. Will someone guide them today or is there no sneak to be seen?"

A low murmur came from the crowd. Then came a hand, but one made of sticks with a clattering sound. "I will take them, sir Rouxx," said the voice. Rouxx must be the name of the robed man, but who was this volunteer?

The figure came through, a boy and one very short. He had hands and arms of sticks, not to mention feet, too.

"A stick boy," Wick said, not just a little bit frightened.

"I'm not a stick boy!" the boy said. "Well, I am. But only half!"

"Half?" Pocket asked.

"They almost turned me all the way," the half-stick boy said. "But the princess broke me free and sent me here with an offer to stay. That was some time ago but I'll owe them forever. I'd do anything to help the princess and her mother."

"Say," Pocket said, eying him close. "You look familiar."

The boy shrugged with a clatter.

"Yes he does, a bit," Wick added.

"We should go now," the boy said, the sooner the better.

In all the excitement Pocket nearly forgot their next mission. "Right! We must get to this valley. We will follow your lead young friend, just show us the way."

"Say, do you have a name we could use?" Wick asked.

"My name is now Twig, though once it was Trouser." He paused a moment, thinking it over. "I think now Twig is much better as twigs live in forests."

"Then Twig it is," Wick said. "I am Wick and she is Pocket."

"Glad to meet you, Wick and Pocket, come with me now, we have much sneaking to accomplish!"

Chapter 17

The Whistling Valley

"So what is it about this valley that we need to be sneaky?" Pocket asked. They'd been walking for minutes now, but if felt more like hours. They'd left Silence, out through the fog once more, back into the forest with its trees and thorns.

"One with an Orsini, of course," Twig said. "Bothering them will get you nowhere fast."

"What is an Orsini?" Wick asked.

"You will see shortly I am most certain," Twig said.

They came to a large vine-covered stone wall, larger than any Pocket had ever seen. Twig felt around and looked this way and that.

"Don't tell me we're lost already," Wick said. "We have business to do."

"No, it's here somewhere," Twig said. "Around here close by is the only way through."

He looked high and low and Pocket could hardly take it. They'd been up and about for so long, her patience was starting to slip.

"Ha! I've found the way in!" Twig said from up on a boulder. "Climb on up and we will go over."

Wick helped Pocket climb up the rock following soon after. He climbed right up on top. Twig led them down the other side and into a small opening in the stone wall. It was only one person wide, and barely one person tall.

But in they went, all three of the sneaks, and once through the opening they stood in the valley down below the hilly peaks.

"Wow!" Pocket said, for it was truly a sight.

"It's time for quiet and quickness now so hush," Twig said, sneaking low through the brush.

Pocket still couldn't fathom what all this sneaking was about, but when they arrived at a small fishing pond she figured it out. There on the bank of this nice little pond stood a giant of some kind which was certainly odd. It had long shaggy hair and big pants dangling to its ankles. But no shoes or socks or shirt to speak of and it was dragging its knuckles.

"What is that?" Pocket said. "Or should I say who?"

"That's the Orsini," Twig said. "He lives in the valley all alone that's who."

"But is he really that scary or is this some silly trick?"

"He is sometimes scary and angry or both, which is why we should be gone from here and on our way quick."

Twig dashed through the forest deeper into the valley. Pocket and Wick sped along to, desperate to keep pace. It was tough going knowing this Orsini was out and about. But sneakily they went and quickly they raced with no time to shout.

When they finally slowed, thinking they were safely away from the giant, Pocket could finally take in the lovely surroundings.

Colorful, flowering trees dotted the valley in every direction. Standing there she could see both sides from here, like two halves of a broccoli split to the core. It was a beautiful place but ever so windy.

"Why must we stand here in this breeze, surely there's a place more hospitable," she said.

"I'm afraid there is not," Twig said. "That's one reason of two this is called the Whistling Valley. For that is why you are here, is it not, to retrieve the song from the stones?"

"I know of no stones, but about the song you are right. Are we close now? I would not like to be stuck here into the night?"

"We are indeed close now, just follow my lead."

They ducked down the hill and headed for the stream. It was just up ahead but something new came into view.

A great circle of stones, stones big as house walls reached up from the earth at varying angles. It truly looked similar to the glass sheets her father could grow back home but of course these were much bigger.

"Whatever is this?" Wick asked, quite curious.

Pocket was speechless, but wondering the same.

"These are the Singing Stones," Twig said. "Our final stop. This is what you are after, now quickly do what you need so we can be free of this place."

"But why? What's the hurry?" Pocket asked, still gazing at the stones.

"Don't you get it, don't you see, this is a thing of the Orsini! He made it long ago to capture the songs, he'll be sure to return if we stay too long."

"But what do we do to find the song? They are just rocks, not instruments."

"Rocks or instruments make no difference. All instruments need one of two things. One is wind, the other is strings."

"Well there are no strings here," Wick said.

There were not, of course, Pocket could see. But there were rocks and...and holes! She saw at last how this was meant to work. Each great stone block had holes running through them of all different sizes. Perhaps they were instruments after all, but now how to play them?

She relayed her findings to Twig and Wick and they all set about trying to learn the trick. But it was the wind itself that gave it away. For when the wind blew just right the stones started to play. A note here and note there it cleverly went, the gusts of winds got caught in the circle and played the full tune.

Pocket shut her eyes tight, listening with all her will and might.

The Thornhaired Princess

She echoed the notes with a hum and a thrill. Three times the wind blew through the whole rhythm and after the third Pocket had memorized it in full.

"I've got it, I think, so let's head back. If the Orsini returns I want him only to see our backs."

"I agree," Wick said. And Twig just gave a nod. They were headed back to Silence, sneaking back towards the wall as quickly as they could.

They heard it well before they saw it. A great panting and grunting coming right at them.

"We must hurry now, he must have our notes," Twig said.

"Our notes? Don't you mean scents?" Wick asked.

"Orsini track by notes not scents. Everyone has them."

"That is unusual!" Wick shouted. "The most unusual nonsense."

They ran and they ran never spotting the Orsini, but they knew it was there they could here its dragging and thudding. When they reached the wall once more they had more trouble finding that door.

"On no, he's almost here!" Pocket yelled and pointed. The Orsini was in sight just at the bottom of the hill.

Twig searched and he scanned, but the opening was hidden. "Where is it? Where is it? We're about to get eaten!"

The Orsini came closer and closer but then it suddenly stopped. It was looking up over their heads at something higher even than its own eyes could top. Pocket followed his gaze up and over her shoulder and found a most thankful sight.

The queen stood on the wall there in all her might.

"Thank you, good queen, as you can see we're in quite a mess."

"Don't worry, good child. The door is here, just to your left."

Sure enough, the queen spoke true. Pocket was thankful again as she reached the part of the forest where she belonged. And behind her came Wick and Twig, following her through.

"I'm glad your back," the queen said. "I hope dearly you've heard and remembered the song."

Pocket nodded and ran through it once in her mind. Then she

started to hum the song given by the stones and the wind as the queen listened along. She hummed stronger and louder with each pass until finally she finished to a happy and smiling queen.

"Thank you, good Pocket, you have kept your bargain. Now I will keep mine. At the stream in Silence's current location you will find a nice boat. Twig, I hope you will help them on the next stage of their journey as well, for they head for the Tower you know so well. You know the way, just as you did here in the valley. Your instincts will guide you and get you to the end. Once you have made it to the Tower I will give you my last bit of aid, for once you leave the Tower you go beyond where I have power. A way to the island you will need and that I will provide. The rest will be up to you to recover what you desire."

"Thank you so much, good queen, we really could have asked for nothing better. And we will return when we are done to see you and the princess again."

"I hope that is true," the queen said. "And for the song I thank you. I must be off now; it is going to be a big day tomorrow for us all. My daughter will be growing and you will be adventuring once again. Take tonight off and rest up well. You have a tough road ahead, though not such a long one as before."

"Goodbye, queen of the Thornwood," Wick said.

"Fair well, good children," the queen said, and with that she was gone, back to her palace and daughter with the new song.

The travelers went to Silence to rest just as the queen had said. Wick fell asleep fast as did Pocket once they made it inside to the town's inn and it's most comfortable beds.

Chapter 18

The Stone Tower

Pocket woke first and headed down the stairs of the inn where only the innkeeper was up and about. He stood at the bar rubbing down the already very shiny wood. Wick was likely fast asleep as he was often very lazy early in the day.

"Good morning, young visitor, you're up quite early!"

"I'm excited to get started, good sir, but also quite nervous."

"I'm sure your trip will go fine. The Stone Tower isn't too far. And the forest that way is safer than most."

"That is good to hear," Pocket said.

She sat at the table as the innkeeper made her some eggs and good sausage. The two boys joined her halfway through her meal, both ready to get going. They ate some food as well as there is nothing as bad as traveling on an empty belly.

After their meal they all grabbed their bags and headed for the river. Once there they found the boat and loaded everything in before setting sail towards the sun.

The boat was lovely and small. It looked simply like a giant leaf, carved and folded to fit them all. It had plenty of room for three; it probably could hold way more. But three is all that set sail from the Silence River shore.

"So what is this tower?" Wick asked as they floated.

"It's just a stone pillar right now," Twig said, steering the boat.

"But long ago they say that's where the sky island first broke free from the rest of the earth."

"So that's why they dock there when they need to land?" Pocket asked.

"I guess so," Twig said. "And it's the only place high enough to reach them at all, any tree or building would be far too small."

They sailed downstream, the boat bobbing right along. It was so peaceful and calm Pocket almost wanted to sing a song. But sitting in the sun was perfect and nice. She could think of nothing more pleasant except maybe lemonade and some ice.

"Ah, there it is, you can see it up ahead," Twig told them.

Pocket joined him up where he steered, she looked out beyond the river, beyond the hills and saw the where the stone tower leered. It was a wiggly and delicate thing, like two legs crossing and twisting up to the sky. It was still far away, so far she could hardly stand it.

"How long until we reach it?" she asked, dreading the answer.

"We'll be able to dock in maybe an hour or two. From there we'll have to walk to the base of the stairs that the curl up the tower."

"We cannot simply dock just right at the tower? I thought the river ran straight through and below it?"

"It does, to be sure, but there is something that guards the river entrance. A great river beast called the Arthex is there."

"Another guardian creature? I thought the queen said it was clear."

"She did, and she's right, but she meant the way up the stairs, not the creature found there. The lake below the tower, to where this river flows, is where the Arthex calls home. The queen would never force any living thing from where they're from. Besides we don't want the Arthex gone from its place as it protects us from those puppets just as it protects the puppets from the woods. It's the guardian of both, keeping each where only the other belongs."

While Pocket was displeased about more walking this day, she agreed that the beast had its right to stay. So on sailing they went

The Thornhaired Princess

the river so calm. She wondered how the princess was getting along.

* * *

The princess sat waiting on the tree palace steps, when her mother returned with a smile and a spring in her step. But the princess was not nearly so pleased. She was silently upset that her friends had to leave.

"Cheer up, daughter, for this is a good day."

"I didn't want them to go no matter what you say."

"I understand that you miss them, I don't like you feeling sad. But they have retrieved the song for you so there's reason to be glad."

"What reason is that, my queen and mother?"

"This song is your future and that of the Thornwood, for it is how you gain your new power."

"What good is this power? I'd rather have my friends back to play and to show them this great forest is where they should stay."

"They will return when they finished, Pocket gave me that promise."

The princess gave a deep sigh and stood by her mother. "Very well, mother, let's get this over so I can try to have some fun."

The queen eyed her daughter carefully wondering if asking the kids to return was the right thing to have done.

The travelers would be reaching the Stone Tower very soon. The queen glanced up to the sky to take a look at the now blue-shadowed moon.

* * *

Twig steered them over to shore, hopping overboard first to help the others out of the little boat. The tower loomed overhead making everything around seem smaller in scope.

"Now we climb the stairs to the top and wait for the queen to do what she will," Twig said.

"How many stairs are there?" Wick asked, looking up at the tower as if trying to count them already.

"No one knows and no one can count that high even if they tried," Twig said.

The Thornhaired Princess

"This is not my idea of fun," Pocket said. "But let's get started so we can be done."

They skipped across the giant lily pads set in place from the shore to the tower's base. Hopping and dashing quickly and with haste. They made it across without any mistakes.

Taking a moment to rest Pocket took a look back at the lake. Down in the water came a shimmering wave like a snake.

"What's that?" Pocket asked, backing away.

"That's the Arthex," Twig said, "What's it doing in water this deep?"

Out from the water came a strange looking creature. It had big yellow eyes and fins like a fish, but also arms and hands like a person, thick and strong like those on a blacksmith.

"Who is here?" it asked, its voice deep and like drums.

"It's me," Twig said. "On a mission from the queen."

"Hmm," the Arthex said.

"What brings you this close to the Tower?" Twig asked.

"Darkness," the Arthex said. Its gaze drifted up and up to the sky.

That's when Pocket saw that the moon had changed, covered in shadows swirling like smoke.

"It's just the moon," Wick said. "It will go back to normal before long."

"Hmm," the Arthex said. "I am scared of this change, that's all I know."

"Then here," Wick said, digging through his pouch. You can take one of these. They're new!" He handed the creature one of the cinnamon gold candles.

"Hmm," the Arthex said. "This is very shiny."

"It has a nice golden light and smells good too."

Pocket wondered why a creature of the river would need a candle that required a flame but didn't say anything. This creature could block their path it seemed, best keep him happy she supposed.

"This is very shiny," the Arthex said. He disappeared

underwater with barely a splash. The children looked to each other, each shrugging aghast. The Arthex popped back up with a fish in its mouth. With a nod it tossed it over to the children the fishing landing with a bounce.

"Take fish," the Arthex said. "Gift."

"Well thank you," Pocket said.

The Arthex left them be as it swam away with the candle over its head.

"That was certainly an interesting creature," Wick said.

"Isn't he?" Twig asked.

"I think he's wonderful, of course," Pocket said. "Though he's quite unusual to say the least."

"Indeed he is both, I would agree. Let's keep going we will make it soon I do believe."

They started up the stairs still carrying the fish. They climbed and they climbed until they could climb no more. Gone was the view of the lake replaced by the view of clouds in every direction. They stepped up onto the last step and found an incredible sight just ahead. There was the island, just a stone's throw away. It had appeared as if from nowhere, but there it was now, so close in view.

"Now we wait for a bit for the queen to do her thing," Twig said. "What that might be I can only imagine."

They had to wait only moments, as if the queen were right there, for something started to happen that made all the children stare. Vines crept up the entirely of the tower, curling and slithering all up the stone. They gathered together at the edge of the tower. Just as the princess had made them a bridge over the small stream to Silence, the queen made a similar bridge though much larger from the tower's edge to the island's nearest ledge.

"The queen is quite magnificent, is she not?" Twig said. "Oh, I almost forgot." He dug around in his backpack as if looking for treasure. When he came up for air he handed Wick a bundle. "This should get you a meeting with the one you seek. But that's as far as you'll get, the rest is up to you in this matter."

The Thornhaired Princess

Wick opened the bundle and found something they had once lost. Not exactly the same, but something they had paid as a cost. It was a puppet, like the one left behind after the tree had been stolen. Though this one was much older, far older than they could imagine.

"Thank you so much, for this and for coming along," Pocket said. "Is there some way to repay you for this and for all you have done?"

"Of course not, good friends. Though I am a bit hungry. Would you mind if I had that fish?"

"Of course not," Pocket said, handing it over.

"Great!" Twig said. "Besides this the joy of helping you and the queen and her lovely daughter is all the payment I need. Now you better get going, before the island once again leaves."

Wick and Pocket gave Twig a hug before running along the great vine bridge. Twig waved them away before starting his return trip down the stairs.

But it was no trouble for him as he meant was he said, he made the trip down with a smile, a fish, and laughter in his head.

Chapter 19

The Sky Island

Pocket realized maybe a bit too late that she should have asked the queen or the princess more questions about the sky island. As they crossed the vine bridge and landed on the other side she discovered she did not know what to expect of this most unusual place and where to go or what to do.

But Wick seemed more confident, marching right along firmly once he stepped off the bridge onto the sky island's solid ground.

"Do you know this place, good Wick?" she asked.

"Not at all, my friend, not even the tiniest bit!"

So walk they did, being careful as they could. They headed through the island's grassy edges towards the shapes looming up ahead. It was the outline of a city, Pocket had learned that from their approach to Vent, but this one was different in some very important ways. First it had only one tall building at what looked like its center. The rest were much shorter, barely making it as high as a quarter way up that tower in the center. And then there was the other shape, one most troubling of all. The entire place was surrounded by a gigantic wall.

They continued their approach until it became very obvious, they were going to have to find a way into a place they would not be very welcome.

"How are we going to pass through this wall when we're not supposed to be here at all?" Pocked asked.

"If there wasn't a passage through the queen would have told us to stay. She led us here so there must be way."

The came to the wall and followed it around. It climbed nearly 20 feet high by Pocket's guess, as smooth as a river stone. They kept the wall at their left as they traced its arc around. It wasn't long before the wall gave way to an even taller gate, with doors of heavy wood and windows covered by iron grates.

"Who goes there?" shouted a voice from above.

"Um," Pocket said, unsure where to start.

But Wick stepped in and said, "We came to return this!" And he held up the puppet that was nearly falling apart.

There came no answer for a good long time.

"Open the gate!" the voice shouted now, to the relief of a shaking Pocket and a shivering Wick.

They were going to get in and finish this once and for all.

The city beyond the gate was something to behold. It was smaller than Vent, but much cleaner as prettier all told. The central tower appeared made entirely of glass, while all the buildings down low were made of all brick or stone with roofs of straw and lawns of green grass. A great roadway led from the gate towards the center. By the look of it the road led all the way through the city to a second gate straight across.

"This place is very unusual," Pocket said. "There's nothing but straight lines without a curve in sight."

"Someone must have planned this for many days and nights," Wick added.

"You there!" shouted the voice from above.

The two travelers looked up and saw it some kind of solider. He wore a uniform that looked quite familiar. It dawned on Pocket quickly that it was the very same outfit that those puppets had worn when they stole her blue tree. She grew a bit nervous then, and wanted to flee.

"Follow this road to the Glass Tower in the center. It's the tallest one," the solider said. "There you can return the puppet to the man in charge."

"The man in charge?" Wick asked.

"The puppeteer of course," the solider said.

"Of course!" Wick added.

The soldier went back to guarding the gate while two friends and travelers scooted down the road and towards their second tower of their quest, this one newer and made of glass.

The closer they came the taller the Glass Tower seemed to grow. It loomed overhead all shiny and clean. There a great many people wandering about town. Though something very unusual about them bothered Pocket quite a lot.

They moved in strange ways with lots of bobbling and jerky movements.

"They're all puppets!" she said as soon as she spotted the strings. Up here on the island she could barely make them out. They were clear like spider webs almost impossible to see. They all came from up high, from a top the tower. She realized now that even the solider had not been a man, but a puppet all along.

"This place is growing a bit silly," Wick said. "Why have a puppet baker there and a puppet doctor over here."

He pointed to both places as they continued on their way. This place was most unusual and strange.

The tower stood directly ahead. It had large front doors, all glass of course. They went inside and up to a desk where more puppets stood as if waiting on their arrival.

"We were told to come here to return this," Wick said, showing the old puppet.

The puppet at the desk looked from it to them. Its large eyes seeming to drink them in.

"Of course, travelers," the puppet said. "We've been expecting you."

The Thornhaired Princess

"You have?" Pocket asked, suddenly quite afraid.

"Of course, follow me. The puppeteer wants to see you right this way."

Pocket and Wick looked to each other. This was most unusual, the strangest of all. But they had come this far to turn around now. They'd see this puppeteer and end this silliness once and for all.

They followed the puppet into an elevator. It pushed a button then hopped out leaving the kids by themselves. "It will be a quick ride to the top, and then you'll be done. Try to relax, I'm told the elevator is fun."

The doors closed to the elevator and Pocket let out a sigh. The elevator started lifting and picking up speed. Higher they went, high into the sky.

* * *

Back in the Thornwood, the queen and the princess stood together looking off to the distance within their woodland home.

"They should be there soon if not there already," the queen said to her daughter.

The princess had been learning the tune Pocket had brought back from the valley and had just about memorized it in full. "Good, that means they'll be back soon."

"Maybe," the queen said.

"What do you mean? They are my friends and they said they would return."

"Maybe, daughter, but there's more to this than just your friendship. The puppeteer may offer them something they could not refuse, something greater than even I could provide."

"What could that be?" the princess asked.

They stood atop the tree palace, the very top of the Thornwood, looking off in the distance. The Stone Tower was faint from here, just a shadow in the distance.

"Never mind that now," the queen said. "You still have a bit of practice yet to do. We will know their decision very soon. Once their choice is made then we'll know what to do."

The Thornhaired Princess

They went back to practicing, singing the song. The princess glanced often off in the distance, growing tired of waiting so long.

Chapter 20

The Puppeteer

Pocket stepped out into the top floor of the Glass Tower, the office of the puppeteer. Knobs and levers covered every wall from the floor to the ceiling, all of them attached to tubes filled with strings. This was the control center for all of the puppets, both those out in this strange city and those that ran away with her blue tree.

"Welcome, guests," the puppeteer said. He sat in a big chair behind a big desk full of buttons and levers. "I've been waiting for you to show up since the day of our theft."

"Where is it?" Pocket yelled, unable to hold it in any longer. "Where is my blue tree?"

"It is here safe and sound, I'll bring it out but first you should sit down."

His voice was surprising as it was light and cheerful, but maybe too much so. He waved them over to two chairs in the room's center. A third flipped up from the floor where he stood across from the weary travelers.

The puppeteer sat and spun in the chair revealing himself. He was young, very young, maybe a few years older than the Pocket at Wick.

The Thornhaired Princess

But his eyes.

His eyes showed he could be wise when he wasn't thieving. It occurred to Pocket just then that this man – this boy – must be a great builder, for he made all these puppets and the city that held them. And of course he had managed to make this island fly! But why did he live here alone without family or friends? Why steal a single tree when he could build a whole city?

"I'm glad you could make it," he said, as if chatting. "I thought that evil queen might trap you there in forest in or maybe her daughter, that thorny haired demon."

"The queen isn't evil, you nasty old thief," Pocket said. "The queen gave us protection and the princess rescued us from roplings and kids made from sticks. You've done nothing at all except steal our blue tree that is precious."

"I guess I forget the truth sometimes," the puppeteer said. "When you've travelled the world like me and told as many lies as I have you forget which ones you've told and which ones you simply believe."

Wick was frowning, Pocket saw and then she understood what the puppeteer truly meant. "It's you! You're the one that tells lies about the queen and of the forest where she resides. But why? Why make up stories about a queen in a forest?"

"She has blocked my way out of this island and this city, keeping me caged up. Now I have caged her as well, keeping people away from her palace in the forest."

"But you're in an island that flies, you can go anywhere your heart desires," Wick said.

"My island floats high above and I can see many things, that is true. But I cannot reach the ground without others coming here. Nothing could be worse than having other people on my perfect island. Why do you think I live here amongst my puppets, over which I have total control?"

"Then why steal my tree? What is it to you?"

"It is a treasure that I wanted and cannot make for myself."

The Thornhaired Princess

"So you just steal it?" Pocket asked.

"Yes, indeed. But it was my puppets in truth."

"But they are controlled by you, you evil man. You are the one to blame, not some toys on strings."

"Of course you are right, how silly of me, but there is another reason for my theft you will soon see. But first I will keep my promise. Bring out the tree," he called, hopping up and over to his desk. He pushed a few buttons then pulled a few levers. The doors to the office opened once more and out came four puppets.

They carried a large glass box. Inside was the tree, though much smaller than before.

"What have you done to my great blue tree? This is just a tiny toy model."

"I shrank it down of course so it would fit on a shelf." The puppeteer looked at the boxed in tree quite proudly. "What good is a treasure that cannot fit in your house?"

"It is a tree not just a treasure, it belongs outside in the sun and the sky. You are a truly evil, evil old man."

"You can have it back and it will return to full size once back in the ground, but first I must tell you the price I demand."

Pocket thought dearly of trying to steal the tree and run. But run where? There was nothing to be done. "Of course, of course, there is always a price. What do you want for the tree, you evil old man?"

Out came a second group of puppets carrying a second large box. This one was wooden and looked ancient and heavy. It had two doors on the front which were locked up tight. The puppets set it on the ground near the puppeteer's desk and ran out of sight.

"My price that I want in exchange for the tree is the memories of your journey here to my island. I would have the story from the theft and when you left and everything after. You would remember nothing of it all. None of your journey here, not even the theft. You would just be home with the tree back home where you belong."

"Our memories?" Wick asked.

Pocket thought of their journey from home to here. Sure there were times when it was scary and silly and she could forget those bridge boys just as soon as tomorrow, but the queen and the princess and dear Mittens she couldn't and wouldn't dream of forgetting.

"See, the theft was just a plan all along, to get you to leave and go on your quest. The true treasure I want is a story I cannot have. I don't ever leave this city of mine. I make no new memories for my puppets to gain. I must invent them when I can but buying them is easier. Inside this box is the doorway for you to forget. All you must do is pass through the doors, the memories will be mine and the tree will be yours."

Wick looked to Pocket who now had tears in her eyes. She wanted her tree to be returned for the town. They had traveled this far the tree was supposed to be their prize. What would Sail do without the blue tree? It would continue to suffer and dwindle from the place it had become. But could she give up her new found friends?

"It's OK," Wick said, quietly. "We'll all be fine."

Pocket felt herself be filled with new strength. Of course the answer was obvious and plain as could be.

"You can keep it, you mean old man, and I'll just make a new tree!"

She got up to leave but the puppeteer stood faster.

"You've made your choice, little girl, but a price you still owe. If I cannot have your memory, there is only one place for you to go. If I don't get a story from you, you can tell no stories of me."

The puppeteer slammed a great button on the top of his desk, the floor underneath Pocket and Wick dropped out sending them falling. Faster and faster they went, racing towards the bottom of the underground pit.

But it was clear to them soon that there was no bottom at all. The light they saw below them was not a light but the bright green earth where they belonged.

They fell and they fell until the island drifted away right above them.

"This is most unusual!" Pocket yelled.

"I agree quite a lot," Wick said. "I guess this is the end, dear Pocket, but at least we will remember our dear friends and they will remember us."

"I'm glad you think so!' Pocket yelled. "I also hope Mittens remembers to keep making wishes!"

Chapter 21

The New Princess

The princess and the queen stood on their balcony, looking up the sky where the sky island soared. It had broken away from the Stone Tower and was headed over the great plain. Even from where they stood, so far below, the spotted the two figures falling down and down and down some more.

"It would appear that they have made up their minds, daughter of mine. They are falling back to the earth without their treasure in tow."

"You mean the price for the tree was something they could not pay?"

"Could not pay it is one thing, but the truth is that they *would* not pay it, at least if I had a say."

"But what was it? What could they not pay to end with this falling?"

"I don't think they knew the result would be falling if truth be told, but the puppeteer steals memories and stories from others now that he's gone rotten and cold. That was his offer, I have no doubt, their memories to go home with the tree, back to how everything used to be, and to forget everything after the theft of their tree."

"So the treasure they sought through this forest and everywhere

The Thornhaired Princess

they had to go, they gave up in order to remember their journey and us and all others?"

The queen gave a single firm nod. "That would seem to be the case, daughter of mine."

The princess looked up at her friends doing their tumbling and watched them falling and falling. It was then she started to sing the song those same friends had brought back from the valley. She sang and she sang until the color of her eyes started to change.

They turned a magnificent green, brighter than a diamond while her hair changed to white like a cloudy, icy sheen. The thorns had changed to flowers in bloom, delicate petals of red, purple, and blue.

When the tune was finished, the princess gazed up to the sky. With a push off the ground and light all around, the thornhaired princess started to fly.

* * *

Far away, back in the city of Vent, Mittens climbed the hill up towards the old wishing well. It was the first time she'd gone alone, the memory of her friends gave her strength she'd not ever known. She peered over its edge and made her wish to protect those in danger. It required a screw, a nail, and the shell of a snail. She tossed them in and waited for the sound of their splashes, then turned and left the well once again.

On her way down the hill she caught sight of the island, floating high over the plain. There was something new there, something she could not explain.

A massive flower, a rose by the look of it, was growing up from the plain, stretching towards the island, rising as high as the tower. It was following a small light, a green fire blazing and soaring through the sky. The rose just kept growing and growing impossibly high.

* * *

Pocket saw the great flower first and the green fire second.

She was still falling but tumbled no more. She had straightened herself out for good or ill. The great rose petals seemed to swell, the massive red petals ready to swallow her as she fell. The green fire spark, the much smaller shape, raced past her at incredible pace. She turned, following its path up and into the island where they'd fallen through space.

"Was that who I think it was?" Wick shouted.

"I think it might have been!" Pocket screamed with delight.

The giant rose stopped growing towards them and instead billowed out. Pocket at Wick kept heading right at it, ready to land amongst the leaves. The fell and they fell until they had no hope to stop, so they gave in and closed their eyes and waited for impact.

Pocket landed first, colliding with the petals. They caught her quite softly like a bottomless sea of feathers. She bounced up a bit and rolled to one side, gliding down the petals, towards the stem inside. There she found an area where she could once again stand, the ground underneath felt truly quite grand.

Wick came next, landing and bouncing all the same. The flower funneled him down landing next to his friend.

"This is a most unusual flower," Wick said.

"Yes it is, it's quite lovely in that way."

"The queen must have spent a great deal of energy getting this here before we hit the ground."

"I don't think it was the queen this time at all," Pocket said. "I think the princess has gained some new powers from the song that we found."

She pointed into the sky as the green spark of light disappeared under the island. It launched straight up into the darkness from where they had fallen.

* * *

The princess paused for only a moment, stopping and waiting to make sure her rose had caught her dear friends. She could see them quite easily, even from up high. Like a great bird searching for prey. Once she saw her friends land and reach the stem of her great rose, she waved a hand for it to lower to the ground.

She had more work to do before joining them though. She

The Thornhaired Princess

raced upward, into the island to return the thing puppeteer stole.

Flying up through glass tower, she broke dozens of windows as she went. She was no longer just the princess but wind itself in some sense. These metal tubes and glass wall her no match for her. She reached the puppeteers office, tearing through the floor.

Looking around the room slowly she searched for the treasure. Ignoring the man staring at her, clearly afraid, he was not important except for the price he had to pay.

She saw what she sought resting on his desk. She walked over and took it, the blue tree in its chest. Without a word she turned and dropped through the hole she'd made in floor, letting herself drop, drifting down and down like a leaf on the wind.

* * *

Pocket at Wick were safe on the ground. The great rose having been lowered somehow. It was only moments later that green spark returned, floating towards them with incredible speed. The light winked out as grew closer and closer. It was clear then they'd been right in their guess. The princess appeared with green light still in her eyes. She set foot on the rose with a nice little surprise.

"My dear friend!" Pocket exclaimed, racing towards the princess. "And my tree! You have saved us all!" Pocket threw her arms around the princess, causing a smile.

"What are friends for?" The princess said, voice like a song.

"You have changed, good princess," Wick said, hugging her as well.

"I have indeed, thanks to the both of you. Come with me now we'll return to my palace. You can rest there with me and my mother and decide what to do."

"That sounds lovely as I need to rest my poor little feet," Pocket said. "Falling through the air is more exhausting than I would have dreamed."

They shared a laugh as they drifted along, the rose carrying them towards the great forest. But there was a thought on Wick's mind that he could not hold in. "What will become of the puppeteer and the island when all is said and done?"

The princess gave a smile quite wry. "My mother has a plan for him, now that he's been caught in the act." She pointed overhead, up to the sky.

The sky island was moving again, but not on its own. It was being pulled by great vines coming from the tower of stone. It seemed the queen was increasing the protection, holding the island in place with arms of vines and fingers of thorns.

Pocket held the little blue tree, smiling again, but it wasn't her treasure returning that was making her grin. Being here now with the memories of all they had done, she knew then that she had made the proper decision.

Chapter 22

The Princess' Plan

Pocket and Wick slept wonderfully that night in the queen's palace, waking the next morning to a large fancy breakfast. There were bowls of berries and plates of eggs, sausage and bacon that was roasted and last of all the baskets of bread that was toasted.

The now snowyhaired princess ate with them which was quite a delight. The queen was absent, though, which Pocket thought was a shame. Pocket had grown to like her a lot from the previous stay.

The three young ones spent the day in the woods, wandering around with the princess as she continued her work. Her powers were quite something you see. Her new hair was just the start, as her changing meant she was almost ready to be queen. Plants grew quickly under her songs, and animals that were sickly soon went back to running along. Whispers and songs she sang to beast and bushes alike, all full of kindness and delight.

"What will you do now?" she asked Pocket and Wick.

"Go home I guess," Pocket said. "The people there need the tree and these are people that I would miss."

"Oh, that's too bad," the princess said. "I very much like when you're here."

"We can always visit as much as you like," Wick said. "We'll just have to find an easier way to get here than those bridge boys and their lies not to mention their crazy old cart."

The princess laughed at that, but also seemed thoughtful. Pocket had no doubt the next time they decided to approach, there would be a bridge waiting for them better than any stagecoach.

Back at the palace the queen stood waiting on the front steps, watching the children draw near.

"Pocket, dear, I would like to talk to you for a bit, if you wouldn't mind."

"Of course, good queen."

The queen nodded and gestured for Pocket to follow. Wick went off with the princess to gather up their belongings.

The queen took Pocket to the bright little meadow where they'd once talked of the moon. She noticed now that the shadow was nowhere to be found. The moon was back to normal, shining green and round. The queen took a seat on a tree stump, while making a seat for Pocket made of mushrooms and roots.

"I would like to discuss your blue tree, my dear Pocket."

"Um, OK, what do you want to know?"

"I am curious as to what it would take for you to let me keep it here, safe and sound."

This was not what Pocket wanted to hear, not all. She knew the queen's intentions were good, but the town needed the tree. But could she really deny this queen who had helped her so much?

"The tree is important to our town," Pocket said. "The material it provides gives our town prosperity and joy."

"But it also brought thieves and danger all the same."

"True enough," Pocket said. "But that should be gone now with the island under control."

"From them you are safe, that may be true. But there will be other evils out there, of that I am as certain as I know the sky is blue."

"Then we'll deal with those too. We have expertise with the tree. I'm not sure what good it would do you."

The Thornhaired Princess

"None at all, really, that is true. It would just be safe here in my forest and give you reason to return."

"Oh, my good queen, you have nothing to fear there. I would live here if my father were here. Wick and I will be back and we'll probably bring others. We've made some friends in our travels that would love to see this magical place. They will believe us when we tell them the Thornwood is safe. Of course we'll have to keep lookout for those stick boys and roplings, but that can be arranged."

"I hope so," the queen said. "My daughter will need you, I feel. I cannot be both her friend and mother. In all things we must do I have to be one or the other."

"Leave the friendship part to us," Pocket said. "You be a mother and queen."

"Excuse me," the princess said. "But I think I have an idea."

The queen and Pocket turned to see the lovely snowyhaired princess standing in the meadow.

"An idea?" the queen asked "An idea for what?"

"For everyone to get what they want."

* * *

They had talked and talked through most of the afternoon. When Wick and Pocket finally headed for home their last little way was under the moon. They carried their things and with them went the still little blue tree.

"Will it work? Wick asked, "This plan with the queen?"

Pocket shrugged for its all she could do. "We'll just have to see."

On their way home they passed by Vent once again. The princess had made for them a nice flying flower that cruised along at good speed, much smoother and safer than that silly bridge boys' cart.

They searched for Mittens at the book-maker's store. It much easier this time, Pocket was happy to find, as she wore no costume to hide her true form.

"My friends!" she shouted when they arrived. "You all looked different, older, but maybe less wise."

The laughed at her joke but then talked of things more serious. They gave a recap of their travels to island and back. Mittens told them of her book-making and showed them what she had finished.

"This is quite lovely and grand," Wick said.

"Yes, the town of Sail could use a book-maker and I know just who I want living nearby," Pocket said.

"Really?" Mittens said. "You mean it?"

"I do, but I understand if you are sad to leave Vent. Your family was here, and we're just your new friends."

Mittens thought long, and thought hard.

"I think that sounds like something I should try. I've been here long enough but I think I'm ready to say goodbye."

The three went back to the cemetery where Pocket and Wick left Mittens alone. Standing at the edge of the graveyard the two of them talked of home. They left Mittens be as the words she said to the ghosts of those that raised her were for Mittens and the ghosts to share on their own.

"Well, they are happy I'm going with you," Mittens said, rejoining her friends. "It seems they've wanted me to leave for quite a long time but knew that I couldn't." She wiped a tear from her eye and Pocket offered a hug.

"We should get going," Pocket said. "We have a surprise."

The cruised over the land and stopped at last in their home of Sail. They were home at last with the tree in hand. The town celebrated their return with a party and music. But their mission was not yet finished.

"We have a question to ask all of you, everyone here in our home. It is a tough decision that everyone must make. You'll have to trust us kids, we know that'll be hard, but our future in Sail will be brighter than ever if you believe what we've been shown."

They told the town the plan the princess had dreamed up. They listened well and discussed it at length. Finally, it was put to a vote. One by one the people of the town put their vote in the bucket. A

The Thornhaired Princess

red stone was a vote of decline, a green stone meant they would follow the plan the children had brought back.

The votes were counted by the butcher, the baker and the brewer and they read off the results to a great loud cheer.

Every stone in the bucket was one of green stone. The town had agreed that the plan the princess had sent was best for all. They all placed their trust in these children who were maybe not children now after all.

Tomorrow all their lives would change, but they'd all be together as their lives turned a new page.

Chapter 23

Advantage of Lies

The day after the vote, the blue tree was replanted back in its original spot in the old house in the center of town. Once in homes soil it grew back through the roof and to its full normal size.

"That's quite an odd place for tree if you ask me," Mittens said.

"It most certainly is," Pocket said. "Which is why it's so perfect!"

"I agree," Mittens said, with a grin. "It's quite perfect indeed."

The two of them walked down the cobblestone road to where Mittens had set up shop in her new home of Sail. She'd taken over the sandwich shop that Viera had vacated. While it was sad to see it go, Pocket was glad that Mittens could use it.

"I guess we should be getting ready for the great move now," Wick said.

He was of course right as the movers were expected at any moment.

The whole town was ready, their things all strapped down tight. Every table and chair weighted down and ropes tied down every item in sight.

They came just as had been planned back in the meadow with the queen. The vines came up from underground, encircling the entire town. They wiggled and wavered stretching up overhead.

The Thornhaired Princess

This time the vines were not for protecting but for grabbing and holding instead.

The entire town was lifted up into the breeze, pulled up like a carrot by its leaves.

Wick looked up as the great vine arm pulled the town towards their new home. "What a sight this will be, for all those around."

"Yes, a town being carried by vines is not an everyday show." Mittens stood with Pocket near the blue tree in the center of town. "I just hope the Thornwood is as nice as you say."

"Nicer, I think, once we're all there. It will be a place to be safe to grow and to share."

The town of Sail sailed along across the hills and grasslands and Great River as well. Pocket could picture quite clearly the faces of the bridge boys and their tricks so silly.

"What a trick *we're* playing now!" Wick said, reading her mind. "This is much better than any bridge they could build."

The children laughed as they continued to soar. The palace would be just ahead now, Pocket knew. She went to the edge to get a better look.

Soon they crossed over into the Thornwood proper, that a green light appeared, soaring up over the town's edge and landing among them. The whole town gasped as the light faded revealing the princess, their friend. Her flowery hair so pretty and her eyes so sharp, she smiled to them all in welcome and signaling their journey's end.

"Welcome home," she said to all. "We're so glad to have you. This is a great day for us all. I am the princess and I'll always be here to help you whenever you need it." She smiled to her friends. "You'll be arriving soon at the place we have chosen. You'll remember it well Wick, and be glad to know we've cleaned out all the sticks."

"Oh, wonderful!" Wick said.

The town came to a stop while it soared in the air. It was set down slowly and gently with a large amount of care. The vines holding it up were replaced by garden flowers. A great ring of them created the border between where their town and the forest now became one. The town of Sail would not be like Silence. They had the privacy they had sought for so long, but Sail would remain open and welcome to all who wish to belong.

The princess stayed with the townspeople to show them around, while Wick and Pocket took Mittens south. "Come on, it's time for the best of surprises you've seen yet!"

Once in place Wick lit a candle, one with a blinding purple flame. The Quiet Ones came as expected guiding the kids to their town.

"We're glad to see you good Wick and good Pocket. Twig has missed you since you left."

"Twig?" Mittens asked. "What kind of name is that?"

Wick and Pocket laughed to themselves. They raced through Silence to the shore with the boats. Twig stood there looking out over the river. When he turned he smiled and waved, then froze as he saw the third figure.

"Mittens?" he asked.

Mittens looked at the boy oddly with his legs and arms of wood, but she saw through that quickly once she saw into his eyes. She fell to her knees and wept quite openly. "My wishes have come true! I cannot believe it! I have found my family and happiness, too!"

Wick and Pocket gave the brother and sister some space. There would be many things to share in the coming days, but this reunion was for them and them alone, two halves of a heart.

***

There was much joy in the Thornwood that day and into the evening. A celebration was held at the palace of the queen. But as all others gathered the queen took Pocket aside, joined by the princess in the meadow once more, just where this whole plan had been born.

"We are glad to have new people in the Thornwood," the queen said. "It feels more like home now than in any time I can remember."

"I think my townsfolk will all agree sooner rather than later. As soon as the trading returns and people discover this place it will become as bustling as ever."

"Indeed it will, which is what I want to discuss," the queen said. "The people of your town will trust you forever, and trust my daughter in time. But never me, I'm afraid the lies have gone on for too long."

"I don't know, good queen, I think people will come around."

"Perhaps, perhaps not, it matters little to me. There is an advantage to the lies that I am only now seeing. When visitors come they will behave honest and true. The old fear of the queen may be a lie all the same, but it can help protect you too. It's like the thorns you see on a flower. They are a danger, there is no doubt, but they're there to protect the flower not hurt the one willing to appreciate their beauty."

"I suppose you may be right, good queen, but the lies will be forgotten all the same. This forest is a place of peace, soon that's all that will remain. But I have to ask, what does this have to do with me?"

"A great deal you see, for you've spent a great deal of time in the forest now and your time now will only grow. You've also heard the same song as my daughter the princess and know it from start to finish."

"I still don't --" then Pocket realized what she meant. She ran her hand in her hair until she felt a small stab on her finger.

The princess took her to the small pond its waters dark and reflective. There in the water Pocket saw them, the thorns appearing all over.

Pocket stood staring, looking at her own stunned face. "But...but how?"

"You are a Grower, my dear, one of us in your power. You are part of this forest. Maybe not by my blood, but in love you are the princess's sister, Pocket, and so in love you are also my daughter."

The Thornhaired Princess

* * *

So the town of Sail grew and prospered, becoming the heart of the Thornwood under the protection of the queen and now the two princesses, one of snowy white hair full of flowers and the other newer, and covered with thorns.

Pocket grew in her skill of growing with thorns spreading in her hair. All the while they were on the lookout for any danger out there. They knew it would come but not this day. This day was peaceful and happy so they sat and enjoyed it to its ending.

For what good is it to have thorns if there is not something worth defending?

The End

Made in the USA
Lexington, KY
05 August 2016